a flock

a flock of birds

kathleen coyle

◆

wolfhound press

First published 1995 by
WOLFHOUND PRESS Ltd
68 Mountjoy Square
Dublin 1

and Wolfhound Press (UK)
18 Coleswood Rd
Harpenden
Herts AL5 1EQ

Wolfhound Press receives financial assistance from the Arts Council/An Chomhairle Ealaíon, Dublin.

British Library Cataloguing in Publication Data
A catalogue record for this book is available from the British Library.

ISBN 0 86327 471 4

Typesetting: Wolfhound Press
Cover illustration and design: Brian Finnegan
Printed by the Guernsey Press Co. Ltd, Guernsey, Channel Isles

Chapter One

The first thing that Catherine Munster saw when they came out of the courthouse was the Felicity hat-shop. She did not know how long she had been standing there when she became conscious that it was a hat-shop — Felicity's shop where Kathleen had her hats re-modelled. She had gone once with Kathleen to have a hat fitted. Madame twitched and pulled and snipped and cut the feutre on Kathleen's head, and then wet it and put it on a model that had been made to Kathleen's measure. It had amused her and given her the sensation of having the skin of somebody belonging to her stretched on the head of a marble Plato or Caesar, Kathleen's hat stretched over the wooden nose of a mannequin that resembled a profile out of a Greek chorus. The hats were tilted at various angles on their velvet stands, something sharp and hard about them; sharp and hard and silly. They became significant for Catherine of the whole meaning of life — headless. Headlong. She stood staring at them as if they mattered, as if they could stretch up on their steel necks and nod judgement to her soul. The judge had said: 'to be hanged by the neck until you are dead.' The hangman was waiting. The hangman was waiting repeated itself in her ears like street music that one does not wish to listen to or take in. It had to be taken in. What a phrase in which to see clearly and feel nothing. She had never felt less emotional in her life. She was like a river that had flooded its own length and lay calm and dammed at the foot of the mountains by which it had passed. She suffered the stillness. Her only wonder was about Christy. She wondered what he was making out of it; if he, too, was like a river flooded and still. No. He was too young. He had not yet come down from the mountains. It was strange that she felt nothing, that there should have been this left to feel and that it should say nothing to her. When she had found out about Valentine going to the bawdy house she had suffered agonies. And now her youngest, her son Christopher, had got himself condemned to be hanged by the neck until he was dead and she did not suffer. She felt nothing. She was looking at hats with a clarity of vision that could have designed them, one by one without looking at them, again for somebody else. It did not matter if Valentine frequented brothels or kept a girl in Windyharbour. They were going to hang Christy. There were hats in the window. A tram screamed by behind her.

Valentine was dreadfully cut up about it; more than any of them. He was mad angry. He was mad angry against Christy's friends, the men he had always hated, yet he went up to them, after Christy had been taken away, and asked them to start an appeal. It was Valentine who had begun the appeal. It had touched her, like the touch of a human hand on stone, when he had gone up to Christy's friends. She felt terribly sorry for him. He was the one she felt had to be protected, and he was the least protectable. Christy was beyond saving. Valentine had wanted to take Christy's case himself, but as his brother it would have been out of the question. She thought that Teddy Redmond who had taken the brief had nearly made a mess of it. He had been slow, heavy as a piece of lead. But perhaps he had shot home as well as anybody. Nobody, not even Valentine, could have satisfied her. Valentine was convinced that Christy was innocent, that he had never shot the man. She had no convictions. In such a moment as this one's convictions had no place. One had to bear the truth. She knew that men, in the name of God, had taken life. Why should a son of hers be an exception?

She tore herself up by the roots and walked down the street to the hotel where Kathleen was waiting. Cicely was there. The girl was suffering tragically. She was torn and afflicted by the turn life was taking. Barely two months ago, when Christy had come to her with the news that he was going to marry Cicely, it was she who had felt stabbed and afflicted at the turn life was taking. Now she was facing his execution instead of his bridal and she felt nothing at all.

The calmness was overpowering. It was like an anaesthetic under which the idea and thoughts of Christy ground away in terrible impotence. Christy was like a winding-sheet on her cold, anaestheticised spirit. She had a sudden desire to be able to tell him that she was not suffering. She was not unhappy. She was not even what you could call troubled. She was just deadly clear. Her thoughts were turning, turning. She must turn them into something, give reason to them, to preserve her from their piling into madness on top of her. She did not feel like going mad. On the contrary she felt excessively sane.

A man separated himself from one of the hotel chesterfields and came towards her: 'Pardon me . . .' She looked at him, as she looked at the hats in Felicity's, 'No! No!' she replied coldly, put her arm through Cicely's and sailed away from him. 'He deserves . . .' she said to the girl, feeling that she was making an eternal joke of it, 'to be refused absolution.' Cicely did not even seem to know that he was a reporter.

Upstairs, in the hotel bedroom, Cicely took off her fur. She threw it down on the white honeycombed bed. Her shoulders looked so slight when she had taken off her fur that Catherine was moved to put her arm about her silently. She regretted the gesture instantly (and in another moment was indifferent) because it was useless to hide that she was cheating the girl as well as herself. The girl knew and trembled in her arms. 'There,' Catherine broke into speech at last, 'try to be proud of him . . . you believe in his ideas.'

The girl trembled more. 'I can't . . .' she blubbered, 'I love him.'

None of them — neither Valentine nor Kathleen nor herself had said that, that they loved him. She looked out, over the head of the girl her son loved, thinking that they had no need. It linked her strangely to him in that instant, the knowledge that expression was not necessary between them. It made acceptance perfect. It made it possible to her to hold up her thoughts to him, knowing that they would not fail him. And it put down all the barriers. See! she could think to him, I saw a spider last night; it was in the corner pane of your window in Gorabbey. It had come in from the ramblers. Bruce was saved by a spider. When the hangman is waiting one may be forgiven for noticing signs and omens. Perhaps it was a sign. The appeal would, Redmond had said, take anything from a week to three. In that time, from a week to three, public opinion might change and the crowd cry for Barabbas. The delay would be terrible for Christy. It would give him time to regret and to create for himself the life he might have lived. She found herself saying, from the other side of the bed: 'You know, Cicely, it may only be a black cloud.' She would have liked Cicely to think that it might pass after all. 'When Christy was a tiny boy of four he asked Kathy: what is that black cloud in the sky? And Kathy said: it isn't a cloud, it is a flock of birds!'

'A flock of birds.'

'Yes, Cicely, it was only a flock of birds.'

'I wish . . .' said the girl bitterly, 'that I could know.'

Catherine was again possessed in her silence. When Valentine had spoken to Christy's friends he had not been able to hide his anger. He had been burning, alive, quickened. 'My God, you bastard, aren't you going to do anything . . . ?' Valentine's anger was right. It kept him on the side of life. She was just as angry underneath as Valentine, but her anger would not come out. It lay in her, drugged, stupefied, wrapped in the winding-sheet. She did not want him to be hanged. She would rather they shot him. It was cleaner. But it did not matter. It would be all one in the end. Christ had been hanged, and the two sons of Mahomet; Judas had hanged himself. The earth became gallows-edged in her mind.

Kathleen came into the bedroom. She shut the door and stood by it. 'The car has come for you Cicely, they are waiting, they expect you to go home.'

Cicely turned and picked up her fur. There was the same obedience in her manner as in Catherine's spirit, an utter indifference that made life mechanical. She said good-bye with her eyes and did not even hold out her hand. 'I shall come round to-morrow morning,' she said simply and went out with Kathleen. Catherine thought — she is fine, she has courage, she is like me — accepting the truth. It was not that women loved sacrifice or glorified in it, drawing strength from it. The strength came right enough, but the love and the glory were absent. Women hated sacrifice as they hate child-birth but they had to face it. They stood up afterwards as the day stands up from the night, washed from the darkness and full of singing birds and the business of life.

Kathleen came back again. 'Valentine has rung up to say that we need not stay in town for the day. They will only allow him and Redmond in to see him. It is necessary for Redmond to see him, and for Valentine.' Catherine wondered if it was true that she could not see him, but she did not question Kathleen. She was glad that they could go away from the hotel. She was glad that they could go home.

And when, later, they arrived home, some instinct took her straight into the kitchen. She had no business there and she rarely went there. She said to Brigid, before the old woman had time to speak, 'Ask Kathleen, she will tell you everything.'

'They're . . . they're going to take his life?' Brigid stammered.

She nodded. The enormous kitchen table was full of deep blue dishes piled with strawberries. One of them had raped the strawberry-beds . . . .

'It was Travers, ma'am. I was going to make jam.'

'I'll make it,' she answered, and sent for an apron. She was grateful for the occupation. But by the time her labour was done she knew that she would never eat strawberries again. They had ceased to be a food to her and had become an exercise in distraction. She would have a new dream now — strawberries. Strawberries fresh, boiling, potted, labelled — 'Strawberry 1919'.

She went in search of Kathleen who was enclosed in her room. She tapped gently and entered: 'Writing?' she asked.

Kathleen gave her a bitter look. 'No, mother, I am not writing. I am taking a dress to pieces.'

Fresh from her experience over the strawberries, Catherine saw at once beyond the denial that she was saving her writing for the future. She looked at the work in Kathleen's lap. She was taking an evening dress to pieces, taking the fragile gauzy stuff to pieces minutely, stitch by stitch. 'What for?' she asked stupidly.

'For nothing.'

'Once when I was a growing girl I cut up one of my mother's best cushions to make a party dress for the washerwoman's daughter, a mite of three, who was going to walk in a Corpus Christi procession. She looked charming, a fairy. I was compensated for my mother's anger.' The compensation had out-lasted the anger by years and years.

'You know, mother, James Joyce says that we have a country that is like a sow that eats its own farrow.'

She was silent again. She did not live in Kathleen's world. She thought of Paris, where Kathleen lived, as a place where Valentine always got through a lot of money, a place where Christy had never gone. No, Christy stayed in the mountains. And now Christy was in prison. She thought of lions in cages, of the Einstein theory — it wasn't so simple after all as an apple falling to the ground, falling — not a sparrow shall fall. There. You could hold to no theory. She brought her thoughts in to what her eyes could see, Kathleen's dark head and her long capable fingers working the scissors, and the tattered finery lying on her lap. A heap of old gold and blue in the lap of the young woman who was her daughter. In another world these three: Valentine and Kathleen and Christy had been her children. Centuries ago.

'Where did you get to to-day, Mother, after we came out of the courthouse?' She did not wait for an answer. 'Cicely said to Val that she would like to marry him before . . .'

'And what did Val say?'

'He was brutal. 'Don't be a romantic fool! People would only say that you had to, and afterwards that you were mistaken!' She put down the scissors and looked at her mother. 'But if she wants to?'

'What does *he* want?' It stung through her numbness that none of them knew his mind, that they had to think for him. Soon, she supposed, there would be no need, but she imagined that for the rest of their mortal lives they might acquire this habit of completing his.

'When Valentine rang up he said that he is bearing it well. He is in fine spirits.'

If she took everything that Val said soul-deep she would begin to believe that Christy was indifferent, no, not indifferent, but exalted, carrying the consequences with the same flame as that in which he had committed the deed. It was incomprehensible to her in Christy. She knew him so well. She could conceive of it lucidly in saints and mystics. She said slowly: 'He may be upheld by some strength that is greater than his own. It would be a relief if he were truly like that.'

'Ah! If he were!'

The wide, enigmatic look that always excluded her came into Kathleen's eyes. She was grateful for it. It became a protection, a cloak, a covering, a redemption. Kathleen took out her cigarette case and the little patent lighter to which Catherine could never become accustomed. There was something so utterly inhuman about it. It was a little machine insect, a sign of life where life was not expected to be. It had become one of her images, lares and penates, on the same shelf of impressions as the narcissus field in the Swiss valley, and the look (which she had returned steadiness for steadiness) of that rat carrying the frog, a bull frog with tightly clenched hands. Like everybody else she had collected thousands and thousands and at odd moments, and in odd places her soul saw and touched them: a colour, an object, a living creature, a movement — like the speed of the French Northern express which was a horror to her nerves, and which she always connected with her mental registration of the last period of her sexual association with her husband.

She went over to Kathleen's window and looked down into the plum-trees. The fruit was small and green upon them, sloe-like and bitter; the grass below them green and lovely, and a thrush was singing. She was old enough to know the earth's habits and that there was no connection between them and human moods. They could happen in unison, especially in youth when the blood was tidal. She looked back at Kathleen, who with her head tilted back a little and in profile resembled her father. She had Luke's gestures, feminine and modified. Thinking of Luke she said: 'I am glad that your father is not here. He would go mad, madder than Valentine.'

'Do you think that Valentine is mad? He has been of more use than any of us.'

'I do not mean that!'

Kathleen understood. She asked: 'Have men less patience than us?' She felt united to her mother in a strong brotherhood as she asked it.

Catherine felt the bond too. It made her cold, as the possession of some talent which is too valuable to be shown easily. She did not answer. She said instead 'Valentine has been very good.' She did not mean good morally but good as in cricket. He had been able to act, to move, to keep something going. That was the difference. Men were bad witnessers.

'Is Valentine coming here to dinner?'

'I don't know.' And it was queer to her like some evil thing that she could think: he won't go to Windy-harbour to-night to the bed of the unknown girl. It made her think of Cicely. The girl was suffering tragically as young girls suffer, and she could do nothing for her. She took confidence in the known element of Christy's girl. It showed her, at least, that room in his life, cleared it for her so that she had no curiosity, no torment about it. And it liberated her son to her. It was remarkable that whenever she had to place herself in relation to Christy over Cicely's head, she felt strong and confident and sure of him. He was close to her, united, so that her thoughts belonged to him as well being possessed by him. She smiled and looked at Kathleen.

'Don't smile like that, Mother! I can't bear it.'

'My dear.' She turned away and her spirit crossed a

bridge between herself and her daughter.

'I know,' said Kathleen gently, begging pardon in the tone of her voice. She went on smoking.

That's just it, thought Catherine, you don't know. None of us know. We are each separated in this; there is no wedging, no spilling over. We are not monkeys.

Kathleen picked the threads off her skirt. She got up suddenly and rammed the pieces of picked dress into a drawer and shut it. She looked at her mother's back questioningly, with wide eyes, and without speaking went out of the room.

Catherine heard the door shut. She did not turn. She went with her daughter down the stairs, into the rooms into which Christy had ceased to come. He would whistle there no longer. She saw him in the gaol. She saw him as a boy in his bathing trunks coming up the beach at Malinhead, landing the salmon at Ferns, leaning with spread brown hands on the Spanish trunk the day she took the flag out that had been made by her grandmother — the flag and the heap of Balbriggan stockings. She could feel the fine silk of the stockings catch on her ragged finger. And now they were wearing silk stockings again — in colours. Summers ran through her, the sounds of games, of laughter and young lifted voices hidden by hedges, the sense — the old woman's sense of youth. She had passed by there, going up her own journey; and, in return, upon the journey of these others whom she had begotten.

It was a circle. A page open in a geometry lesson. It meant as little or as much as you made of it. You could sit in it as in a dark room and breed all sorts of blacknesses, or you could go out into the open and let the weather catch you. You went by trams and ferryboats or taxis. You arrived. You got what you went for and came back with the packet in your hand — a new book or a crucifix or flowers for the table. Anything. Your limbs moved and you had to use them. But within you the mystery was not always obedient, not always there, absent. And the absence was heavier than the presence.

Valentine came back for dinner. They had cold chicken

and asparagus and there were strawberries on the table. Catherine moved the dish of strawberries towards Kathleen: 'Do you mind putting them lower down where I can't see them.'

Valentine stared. He said: 'Redmond is as hopeful as I am. I am certain he never did it.'

'Did Christy tell you he never did it?'

Valentine renewed the stare at his mother. 'No, but he has never said that he did do it.'

'He pleaded guilty.' Valentine, she thought, was laying too much stress on Christy's lack of reiteration.

'Redmond was a fool to let him.'

Kathleen's hands were clasped in front of her empty soup plate.

'It's this horrible idea of giving up your life . . . of believing that anything can progress . . . it is quite a creed to be born to die in this country . . .'

Valentine interrupted her: 'Oh, don't be clever, Kathy, it isn't the moment.'

Kathleen went white under her brown skin. Her blue eyes shone like stones. 'I know,' she said, in the same tone as she had used a little while before to her mother.

Well, if you know, don't do it.' Valentine took another helping of soup. 'I'm in a hurry. I'm going out afterwards to see Leslie. He could move things with the Home Secretary.'

'And I don't suppose that you've asked Christy's permission to do that?' It was a sort of joke to Catherine, an echo of a joke that was rung on the wrong instrument — not a joke because it had been rung on the instrument.

'Good God, no. I'm not such a fool as all that.'

It did not matter whether Valentine asked Christy or not; whether he spoke to Leslie or not. He was quite right to speak to Leslie, of course. It would have been wrong not to. There it was. Catherine looked at him as if she could not understand. 'Have you seen Cicely?'

'No. Not since this morning. I'm going to see her after I've seen Leslie.'

'All those miles . . .' Kathleen began.

Catherine's mind worked: 'It isn't strawberry jam with

him. I'm glad, Valentine. It is very hard on Cicely.'

'I can't stand when she laughs,' Valentine said it a moment, 'it gets on my nerves.' Nobody spoke and his mind went back a move: 'It's no distance in the car ... I've been driving like hellsblazes to-day.'

'Well, don't get arrested,' Catherine felt herself going off on another joke, 'one is quite enough.'

'Mother!'

'I hope you have your licence?' she asked stolidly.

'Oh dear!' broke from Kathleen. She caught her breath as the door opened and Travers came in. They each looked round at him but he had nothing but a pile of plates in his hand. His entrance preserved them, restored them. They scarcely spoke again.

It was nearly two o'clock in the morning when Valentine got back. Catherine came down in her bedroom slippers when she heard the car. She said nothing to Valentine's: 'What, you up, Mother! It's the middle of the night.'

They turned into the dining-room. She waited while he mixed a cocktail. His eyes had black circles and the corners of his mouth were blue.

'I asked Leslie if he'd go and see him. He said he'd be damned first.'

'But he is going to do something.'

'He'll do what he can. He thinks he's more culpable than anybody and ought not to be let off.'

'You did not expect him to have any other sort of thought.'

Valentine mixed another cocktail: 'Have a cocktail, Mother?'

'I don't need one . . . and Cicely?'

'We went for a walk in the park ... she wanted to know everything that he did when he was a little boy. I told her that we fought like tigers, except when we were united against Kathy. That was all. We talked about birds. She had a baby owl once, a Grand Duke . . . she bred mice for it.'

That was a door by which Cicely could not enter in — his childhood. It led to a kingdom. It was stored with images. He had been circumcised late, when he was five. In Africa Luke and she had met the tall native youths, marching very upright and carrying palms on their Day of Circumcision, their day of manhood. The air was dry and full of fresh warmth. It was there that they had all got their brown skins. They had to give Christy a dreadful lot of chloroform, it had taken ages for him to go under, and he had come out quickly and played with the wooden mallet on the window ledge. His bed was quite close up against the window, where he could see into the orchard. He had played with the Chinese bricks that Mitchell had sent her when Valentine was a baby. The doctor had said to her: Mothers very rarely pay enough attention to the sexual development of their sons. It is left to the fathers. Daughters were different. One knew all about them. One was able to say: Don't mind when you are moody, Kathy, it is a sign something is coming. They all had a trick of leaving their bath-scrubbers in the bath, one after the other. And then they reached a stage when they had a mania for separateness. Nothing was allowed to touch. The clean, sweet-smelling fastidiousness of youth.

Valentine was looking at a folded scrap of paper in his hand. His expression was abject: 'I'm fearfully sorry . . . Christy gave me this for you.'

She took it and unfolded and read it: 'Dearest Mother, don't fret. I'm all right. Look after Cicely. I hear that you are coming to see me with her to-morrow morning, Christy.'

'He scribbled it for you just as I was coming away and stuck it into my pocket.'

He had no right to act like a king towards her, a king instructing his ministers. Look after Cicely. It put such a distance between them, maintained him far away there amongst others. And it was stupid. Cicely was neither a baby nor a ward in chancery. None of them, in this, could look after another. She looked at Valentine angrily. 'I suppose you do mean to go to bed?'

'Yes,' he said tiredly, 'I shall just have another cocktail.'

Up in her own room she opened the windows wide, both of them. It seemed to let in the moonlight better. A green full moon, lying amongst the dark grapes of the night, the dark rounded tree-tops and the dark distant mountains. The sea breathed in the night, up and down, near and far, distance from distance. The deep fruitful womb of the earth was at peace, reposeful, letting every grain make its effort. She stood in the stillness, neither of it nor apart, but numbed on the edge of her own soul, belonging nowhere, nor to herself. Was Christy watching this moon? Could he see it? Feeling was a realm through which she had passed and would never traverse again. She had carried her babies there, loved Luke and given herself to him. She had served her children's infancy. That was her own world, her own intimate minute world. Now she was in the world of others. Everybody. Where Kathleen lived in Paris and mixed with queer people. She found it difficult to value Joyce. Kathleen blamed her for it. She did not say anything, only just looked away and her eyelashes were scornful. But Joyce had begun so differently — in another climate, amongst heavenly wings, layers and layers of ecstasy. Like Lucifer he had fallen into this life. He had not been born like other people, and he had never been re-born. He walked amongst the ashes, knowing so destructively that they were ashes. There were flowers too. When Kathleen stuck the rose into Valentine's face and said, 'smell,' Valentine had said: 'what are roses for?' 'It is a lovely thing,' Kathleen answered, and he sniffed. At seven. The male at seven. Joyce was so often male in the sevenths. You grew out of everything — sight, touch, smell.

And in this world Christy had shot a man and they put him in prison. A life for a life, tooth for a tooth, eye for an eye. It was none of these things. It was death for death. The multiplication in eternity. Eternity came often into her mind. Why? She was on the edge, the gallows-edge with Christy.

The raven heads were folded under the blue-black wings. Better be a bird and wild.

She went, at last, to bed, gliding into the cool linen. She

had no right when Christy was deprived. But that was all nonsense, the sort of nonsense that labelled women with a love of sacrifice. She did not love sacrifice. A waste in the name of heaven was no less waste. It was that that she resented, his waste. To him it was a heroic purpose. Heroism or martyrdom was the fashion. What fools they were these young men, these weavers of wreaths! Other brows bore the thorns. The real sacrifice went to Cicely. She saw that. She could not help seeing it although she knew that Christy would be no longer there. It was just his not being there which proved it. Women had to think it all out for a very long time afterwards. It was useless to blame women for their calculation, for their powers of saying thus and thus over and over. Women went through more evolutions than men in a life-time. They were children, boys, men. It was when they became men, at the end, that they understood men, especially the young men. They looked at them with long eyes of comprehension, seeing them as they never had been able to see them when they were young women. Young women missed a great deal; they were all feelings, instincts, and mistakes, and at the mercy of love. Poor Cicely!

She slept. She dreamt of a ship in a black, frozen sea. The sky was black above it, descending, terrible. She saw the land, ploughed, the earth thrown open and unsown. A badger crept through the desolation and dark hungry dogs ran on the scent. She was afraid, terrified that the earth would break in the blackness and perish. Then out of the silence that was close as death itself broke the rhythm of wings and a flock of birds flew in the sky. They were black. They resembled ravens but their wings had the close serried plumage of owls whose flight is silent. They soared above the ship, dipped and turned over and became white, so white that they broke the blackness. Their rhythm was perfect in its whiteness; it ran like a full sea in great beating waves through the darkness.

She awoke, strangely reposed from this nightmare.

It was Saturday. The day after Friday — Christy's Friday. To-day she and Cicely were going to see him.

Kathleen came with them, and Valentine drove. It was so familiar, yet she was aware as for the first time of the descent from the mountains into the low fine road that ran, corn-edged, for miles into the city. The silent desolated water-mills; the little kraal-like human dwellings. The thick foliated hedges packed with mistrusting bird-eyes. Certain trees were her friends — the Lucan ash and the Madman's sycamore and the copper beech that was a spoilt Egyptian in the midst of the fertile tribes, but to-day they were trees and had the shape of trees. The flint heaps at the roadside meant as much to her. Looking down over the Carybridge into the shallows she saw the gleam of brown trout. Christy would land no more salmon.

Cicely was there, waiting. The gaol gate. She thought of Mitchell teaching her Chinese. He had drawn an arch with a gate shut in it and he had translated it: — shut. He had drawn an arch with the gate open and translated it: — open. The gate was shut.

Kathleen kissed Cicely: 'I'm not coming in, dear girl. I only want to be here when you come out.'

She did not kiss Cicely. She knew that Cicely understood when she didn't and only put her arm through hers. Cages and cages and lions in them. The forest unforgotten. Unforgotten forest. It was better to be hanged by the neck until you were dead than to live in prison. Nobody *lived* in prison. Valentine said: he is in fine spirits.

The cell was not a cage. It was not ventilated. Her thoughts and breath both choked together when she saw Christy's head, tousled. Had he no comb? He came close against the grill and his fingers reached out to Cicely. His eyes reached out to Cicely, glanced, heavy with love to Catherine and went back to Cicely. His whole body leaned towards Cicely, pressing her through the wall. Love burned up out of his presence and Catherine, watching him, saw everything — and that he was not ready to die. Valentine was blind; he was safeguarded by his own thoughts. She had no refuge. She saw the truth. He was not indifferent, he was not burning in flames of exaltation. He was not ready. 'Die at the right moment,' Nietzsche said, as though youth were full of God-like certainties. Madness was necessary.

'Mother!'

'Yes, dear.'

His fingers touched her cheek. 'Don't mind . . . try . . . .'

She stopped him from being stupid. 'Give all your thoughts to Cicely,' she said steadily, and stopped there. He belonged to the rest of them, belonged to the nest from which he had already flown. He was no more ready to die than any young thing that had begun to fly. Far away in her mind she saw a nest and her hand going into it and feeling it warm. And away down, in her, a pain came, a beginning as when you begin to take off a bandage. *Pansement*, the French said. She suffered depansement standing there witnessing this son and the girl he loved together. She had passed her right moment. 'Valentine is full of hope,' she said into their waiting for her to speak.

'Yes, Chris, he believes that you never did it.'

The tremor had lessened in Cicely's voice.

Christy's smile came into Catherine's eyes and drew a smile back with it. They were united. In the same beat. She no longer felt Cicely. Cicely took nothing that she wanted. She would rather now that Christy looked all the time at Cicely. She stood silently, listening, hearing indifferently.

'I'd rather you'd think of me having done it for something we believe in.'

What a child he was! And Cicely encouraging him. Did they truly believe it?

'But of course I never think otherwise.'

'Brave girl!'

'All the same . . .'

'You hold on to Valentine!'

How cheerful his voice was, as though he was going to a game.

'Mother, you'll give Cicely lots of my things, she wants to have them . . . that is, if I shan't need them myself.'

'Why, of course. She must choose . . . if it is necessary.' There! She was playing the same foolishness. It was an umbrella in the rain, not false . . . just an umbrella. 'Christy,' she said suddenly, 'I'd love to send you a tube of toothpaste and a new toothbrush and I'd love to wash your face properly and comb you . . . .'

'And give me a shave!' he sent the laugh to Cicely.

They were nearly happy for a moment. And then Christy's hand rummaged through his hair and the gesture was hopeless to Catherine. It was true. He only had a few more days. It made her go. 'I'm going,' she said.

'Oh, don't go yet!' Cicely cried.

'Yes, I must. But you needn't.' She made it seem as though it were an arrangement for them to be together. She said good-bye as though everything were all right, that he was forgiven, that she understood, that he was a brave boy, that whether she agreed with him or not she was proud of him. And she would give Cicely anything, do anything he asked.

But outside in the corridor she said sternly to the man in uniform: 'Leave me. I shall wait here.' And when he looked at her a second time and then a third time as though she were going to take hyoscin, she said: 'The smells are terrible, enough to demoralise the whole pack of you.'

The man shrugged his shoulders and was impertinent: 'Good enough for the . . .'

She stopped him, Nietzsche vague in her mind: 'Human. All too human. Animals in the earth are cleaner.' Man was the only animal with consciousness and he made hell out of it. She turned away from the man's face, degraded by seeing it. She walked to the corner and where the steps showed she came back to the man, accepting him. She had, in that brief length of corridor, gone over the border into his acceptance. She looked at him, fixedly, with full-seeing eyes. He stared back at her sluggishly and as though he was accustomed to it. She thought that she had never said to Christy that she would see him again. They would let her see him again. They! This man! She would see him again. She would see him millions of times as she had seen him yesterday with his eyes closed. The judge's voice droning like a rabbi's. They burnt black candles at the excommunication of Spinoza and held them dripping over vats of blood. Men liked judgement. Boys pulled off legs and wings. Pain! Pain! It was a pleasure. She was sating that lust, spreading her spirit out into the universal element in which it was abated. The still purgatory souls of women. The sieve through which sin was filtered.

Kathleen was at the foot of the stairs, sitting on a bench. A beam of sunshine cut her in two. The section with the part of her skirt and legs looked droll to Catherine and brought her to her senses. The man's face was no longer duplicated and reduplicated. She saw Kathleen sitting on the bench above and below the sunbeam. She stood on the stone steps becoming conscious of her daughter, coming out from under the anaesthetic, out of the winding-sheet into the full knowledge that Christy was not ready to die. She put it away for she heard Cicely telling the man above that she could find her own way. She waited for Cicely and pushed her past her on the steps so that she came between her and Kathleen.

Cicely said: 'We have seen him.'

Kathleen looked and waited. Tears came into her eyes. They walked out of the gaol, out of the weight, into the street.

'He said you are to come next time.'

Kathleen answered that she would like to.

A voice said white cherries. A newspaper had blown loose on the pavement. They walked round it. The street was multiplied as the man's face had been multiplied.

'What are you going to do, Mother?'

The street melted away. 'I . . . Kathy . . . I'd like to have the car and go home. One of Valentine's men could drive me.'

'Let us ask Valentine,' Kathleen said and they turned towards his rooms.

The car was there. She waited. Cicely and Kathleen went in together. Valentine came down to her. 'You'd better not have Flynn, Mother . . . going out on my licence. We'd better be careful. I'll take you in the car to the garage. One of the Cash's men will drive you.'

He saw her into the Cash taxi, and waved good-bye to her. She was alone. The car ran through the same corn-edged

road, past the same trees to Gorabbey. She got out at the
lodge and walked up. She had the feeling of having got up
very early and walking alone down a country road to catch
an early steamer or train. She felt very alone, very awake.
The garden, even the air, had something unusual about it,
as though she had caught it out of custom.

Travers asked her if she would be in for lunch and she
said yes, but to give her what there was without asking her
about it. She thought Kathleen was coming back in time, but
she was not sure. There was a telegram from her cousin
Mitchell. She put the telegram back in its envelope. It made
her think of Mitchell, wish he was there. Travers was still
waiting. Through the window beyond she had a glimpse of
the artichoke fountain set in the blazing circle of geraniums.
The water wasn't running. She made an effort to dismiss
Travers: 'I'm going up to the oriel . . . you can ring the bell
on the steps . . .' It was Mitchell's telegram that had put the
oriel into her head. It was a tiny stone-walled room at the
top of an outside flight of stairs. She had to go through the
flower-garden to get to it. Long ago, before her marriage,
she used to go there often to think of Mitchell.

At nineteen Mitchell had gone out to China with the
Harps. He had married Mary Harp. She always knew he
would. He had written to her — his first letter: I wish you
were here, Cathy. It is prison without you. I feel shut in,
limited. Mary Harp is like you but her eyes turn up at the
corners and she hasn't your smile. She is my age. The
Chinese are queer, like bamboos stuffed with human
organs. They never answer you. They reflect you. They
fascinate me. They make me want to see from their side,
very still and fixed and rooted like something at the centre,
knowing you could go no further, only backwards again . . .
I wonder if I shall ever know things at the centre . . .

She knew the letter by heart, as well as she knew
Tennyson's poems. She said it over to herself before she
reached the steps and her thoughts dwelt on Mitchell as she
ascended them. All through her life Mitchell had been in the
background. It was natural that he should send a telegram.
His eldest boy had been eaten by sharks in the Pacific. And

now he was with his daughter and grandchildren. They were playing tennis at Santander.

From the door and the top step one saw down into the nests of the ravens. The air lay in dark shade in the trees and through it one saw right to the sea. The glimpse of sea was enclosed as water in an Italian picture. She closed her hands together and looked down over the high balustrade over the familiar scene, and it seemed to her that she was looking down over her whole life, from childhood to the present, and that she had really come to the end. There was nothing more to learn. There was a limit. There were lands she had never seen, snows and deserts, strange animals whose ways she would never know, tongues she would never hear, peoples with souls cloistered in hot or cold solitudes whom she would never reach. What of it! It had been intense to her. It had burned, flamed, blackened and died.

Her children had grown out of her, taken root in another garden. Thought was catachrestic. It mixed its images, not mixed them but saw the truth through layers and layers, lenses.

She had nothing more to learn. She would come back, like the peasant who had never moved, to God. And God could allow these things to happen — could take Christy whose life had only begun and leave her who had ended. It was wrong. It was not the right way to look at God . . . .

It wasn't God. It was life. It was not the right way to look at life. When one was in Rome one had to do as the Romans. She had come down there from youth — from Christy's mountains — to do as the Romans. It had been a defilation. He had escaped the defiling. He was dying at the right moment; at twenty-one, with one thing well-done and nothing undone; the way poets die young — the song fresh and lifted and never remade. He was in her arms when she thought that, folded and safe. He was in her womb and she enclosed him again. She would preserve him into the death he was going to die as she had preserved him into the life that he was not going to live. Experience swelled in her, gravid. And within it, through it, she shared herself with

Christy. See, she thought to him: for you everything has gone; for me everything has gone. I have come out through love into its effacement. This was not love that she was feeling but something greater than love, something that might have been Mitchell's centre, a consummation, a fire in which her own heat answered flame for flame.

Agreement and disagreement were twin hailstones melting as they fell.

She was so close to Christy. Her thoughts opened as doors opened and he could go through every room, on and on until her house was finished. Outside she would hold the house in her hand, as St Brigid held the church. The house would be very little known and they would be able to hold it in her hands.

It seemed dark in the little stone-walled room for a moment. Hyacinth the Holy had written the Black Poems here: Dark the Sea. Dark the Soul. God-wiped well. The Dark Sea and the Dark Soul . . . impossible to translate. Mitchell had studied here out of old Sir Terry Harp's Eastern grammars. She had waited. He had gone away and she had given up waiting. On a shelf at her hand, amongst a row of red German books, she saw a thin black line of passbooks, housekeeping books that she had kept since her marriage. It seemed incredible to her now that she could ever have made all those entries. Butcher, baker and candlestick maker. All gone now, long ago, under the oranges and lemons arches. The passbooks had been brought here amongst her books, after Luke's death. This was her real home. She had never felt truly at home in any of the houses that she had shared with Luke. And it was here (on a visit — he had arrived sooner than he had been expected) that Christy had been born. Yes, she thought to him, you do not know how much of your life has been mine. He had been inside her, inside her life. Soon he would be outside. He would be able to look down at the little house of her life in his hand . . . .

This was Mitchell's centre. The knowing that there was no going forwards or backwards. She stood, absorbed, motionless, seeing her son as she had seen him a little while ago, ramming his hand through his hair. His eyebrows were crisp and young, the pigment raven-black in him.

They were ringing the bell in the garden, ringing, ringing. She wished the bell would stop ringing, that she had not told them. They were even coming up the steps to her. Valentine showed in the doorway, cut against the trees. His face had a scared expression. It made her smile at him, pitying him his imagination. She said in a more normal voice than she had used for hours: 'I didn't know that you were coming.'

'No. I . . . I had a notion that I ought to have come back with you.'

His meaning was confirmed to her. She smiled again, gentler. It was so wide of the mark. 'My dear Val!'

He was caught out. His eyes tried to hide it. 'I say. We've brought Cicely back with us. She wants to go collecting signatures with Kathy. She can't, you know . . . and Kathy doesn't want her. She just can't, you know . . . can she?'

'I see. You'd like me to keep her?' It wasn't a ruse. She understood why neither he nor Kathy could go collecting with Cicely.

'Well, could you?'

'If she'll stay.'

'Can you think of something to make her?'

She could think of nothing at the moment.

She gave Kathleen an understanding look as they sat down. Kathleen was going to ask various well-known literary people to sign the appeal petition. She had already been to Russell.

'He did not know who Christy was.'

'That doesn't surprise me . . . why should he?'

Kathleen, she could see, had expected him to know who she was.

'He is full of the trouble in the Northern shipyards.'

'He would be,' said Valentine laconically, and there was a pause, like the holding down of a minim — small but with its own meaning. He said, as it lifted: 'I see Foch is wading into him . . . he ought to have had the chance earlier . . . .'

That they could, even on the border, speak of the war,

marked the certainty of Christy's absence. War, civil or otherwise, was never mentioned when they were all together. To have mentioned it would have been a species of arson in that atmosphere. Cicely was saying nothing. She was forgetting them. As if, thought Catherine, any of them, by merely talking could forget Christy. She again had that strong, over-Cicely's-head feeling. It made her say to the girl: 'I hope, Cicely, now that you are here, you will stay with me . . . at least until the end of the day?' All the cheating had gone out of it. She was natural again, widened into an initiation that made none of them significant to her. She pitied them terribly.

'Oh . . .' Cicely began and looked, distressed, at Kathleen.

Catherine saved them both. Her voice was gentle, the pity in it: 'My dear, if you stay I will show you Christy's things.' It only just came into her head in time.

The forgetfulness vanished out of Cicely. Something alert, like the light in a little animal that can now come out safely, shone through her. She said simply: 'I should like that better than anything . . . unless . . .' She looked, with an echo of the distress, to Kathleen.

'No,' said Kathleen, 'I don't.' And when Cicely's eyes were down again, she cast a glance at Valentine that said they had got through the turnstile.

Immediately that she had said that she would show her Christy's things the cheating came back. It was going to be terrible to her: one thing on the surface and a different meaning underneath. Subterfuge. The opposite of refuge.

They had coffee in the garden. Somebody, Valentine probably, had turned on the water. The bright crystals of the falling water splashed sparks into the geraniums. The scarlet velvetty petals were full of tears. Teazle, the setter, lay stretched like dead on the lawn, feeling the heat. No bird was to be heard. Butterflies flew silently and listlessly. Catherine, drinking her coffee, saw down into the minutely cropped turf, packed with trefoils. St Patrick and the Trinity . . . asphodel on a cliff in Brittany. Bare feet on asphodel . . . and no floor of heaven, only the very peasant women with dark Mozarabic set eyes.

'You can do it,' Valentine was saying, 'in exactly forty-three minutes.'

'Or spend the night here,' Kathleen suggested.

'They would not . . .' Cicely said, 'like me to do that. Uncle Felix would come out here to fetch me in the middle of the night.'

'It is funny . . . what is one man's meat is another's poison.' Kathleen's voice had a bitter twang in it. 'We are not poison to ourselves.'

Cicely's expression went forgetful again, withdrawn. Valentine was cupping a match against a cigarette; over it his eyes caught Catherine's and gave her a tired tenderness. He looked as if he would have liked to say something, but did not say it.

Kathleen had a sullen air of carrying it through. 'Although we are always having epidemics: now here, now there.'

Valentine said: the tenderness had dropped out of his eyes into his voice (he was looking at Cicely's bowed head), 'Don't, Kathy. It's a good country to pass our childhood in.'

Kathleen got up suddenly and went over to Teazle. The dog did not rise. He wagged a lazy, recumbent tail at her. Catherine had a queer, utterly new, uncontrollable pride in her as she watched her cross the lawn. The girl would be truly beautiful in her maturity. She had the strength that ripens only in the middle years. The best would come out of Valentine and her about the forties. It made her believe in them in a different way, see them clairvoyantly. They each had that black hair that silvers beautifully, and the bodily grace that goes upward suddenly before the final descent. She began to think of Christy . . . if he lived, and stopped herself. She wondered suddenly about Kathleen's unknown love affairs. She was sure she had them. How far they got was another matter. You could never tell with Kathleen. Her sons were known to her. Books of revelations. But her daughter was closed, closed as a Carmellite in her intellectual world. Cicely was sitting between her and Valentine. Her sprigged dress came out clear against his dark blue suit. She was like a shy, amber-eyed fawn in colouring and everything. She put her cup down on the grass. Poor little fawn. She saw her love for Christy as a fawn trapped against the fences, every heartbeat showing. They wouldn't kill her. She would live, and know fright all over again. Valentine stood up. He was going. It would soon be the moment to say 'come' to Cicely. Catherine stood up too. She felt rested, as though she had been asleep.

'Are you coming, Kathy?'

'Coming!'

They all, followed by Teazle, moved back to the house. Catherine was in front. She had a moment, as she entered and turned, waiting, when she felt (seeing the three young forms abreast) that they depended upon her. Their dependence was a relief to her. It steadied and deepened her. She had gone through a door that they had not yet reached.

Kathleen separated herself and stooped, one foot turned over. 'I am going to change my shoes.' She looked up and met Catherine's eyes. 'I am going like this . . . in this dress. Does it matter?'

'My dear, why should it matter?'

'I'm glad . . .' Kathleen glanced after Cicely who had gone in with Valentine. 'It's bad enough by itself . . . .'

'But the poor thing . . .' Catherine said gently. Kathleen interrupted her.

'We are all poor things.'

She couldn't have that. 'We are his own flesh and blood.' She was utterly unprepared for Kathleen's quick arm round her shoulders. She thought wildly: 'I hope she is not going to cry.

'Oh Mother! You are rather splendid!'

She was silent and Kathleen's arm dropped.

'You've changed since this morning, since you saw him . . . you feel better?'

'If you like,' said Catherine, drawing her daughter close to her so that her own face should be hidden, '. . . you can call it . . . that.' It was, in that moment, unbearable. She held Kathleen very tight until the moment passed. They followed the others mechanically into the drawing-room.

Cicely was standing by the French day-bed and she was looking up at Valentine as though she had asked him a life-and-death question. It seemed to Catherine that there was a blue haze in the room, that every movement was moth-like. They were minute like moths. The chairs were blue against the small flight of their thoughts. It was Cicely's moth-coloured dress.

The drawing-room came clear. She was alone with Cicely.

'You . . . you are going to show me something of Christy's.'

'I can show you his outward possessions,' she felt like saying but did not. Instead: 'It was a somewhat rash promise . . . .'

She was prepared for the appeal: 'But you will?'

'Dear child, they can mean so little . . . but, of course!'

There was a deliberateness about their going upstairs to Christy's room, the room that was so indisputably still his, that drenched Catherine with remorse for ever having suggested it. She had done it to save them from each other and from the war and strikes and the edge of nerves that were too ready to feel. Her own nerves were only coming out of the ether. She was strong enough now to hide them. And besides, they didn't matter now. She had got quite beyond them. They were 'there' only when others felt. It was so hard for them all, and for this poor child who so clearly did not know what to make of it. The flood of her morning meeting with Christy came back on her towards the girl who was depending on her — the girl who thought that she loved him more than any of them. She loved him sexually — with desire. She could not help that. The other love had not yet sprung in her. It sprang only from experience — long experience with strange and sudden deeps in it; a sick child . . . financial loss . . . departure after three years' residence, even the natives feeling that something was broken . . . all sorts of things went into it. Understanding. It was built brick by brick, like every other thing.

But the love that sprang from desire! That was worse as it could die from the refusal. The body could die. The body, one knew afterwards, long afterwards, didn't matter. It was the other death . . . the death at the centre . . . .

Cicely leaned forward, quicker than she, and opened the door. The sudden draught from the open door bulged the curtains out towards them and when the door shut the curtains sagged gently back to flat again. The curtains were still. Their immobility seemed to carry in it another sign of Christy's absence. The room was empty to Catherine. It was Christy's room but he was not in it. To the girl it was also Christy's room and it had a significance, an intimacy, a close unsatisfying touch that made her heart break. She turned to Catherine with a little moan.

It was the room of the young man whose bed she had promised to share, and would never share; whose life she had promised to share and which was now being whipped from her. Whipped from her by the leash of the faith they shared.

'Oh! . . . I . . . you, you have had . . .'

'Yes,' said Catherine quickly, covering her. 'But be thankful my dear girl, even in . . . this, for what you have. Nothing, you know, ever comes that does not make us feel.' She felt terribly, nakedly sincere. She wanted to reach through the muddle of the girl's emotions, to solace her at the roots. It was like reaching through to another state, to a youth which she sharply remembered had been incapable of knowing solace. In youth the blood was tidal, the streams muddied. The water had to run and run. She was neither cold nor unsympathetic, but to the girl's age she knew that she appeared aloof. She was the mother before the bride. The young man between them. She was afflicted and then eased by a quick analgesia that took the place of power. 'See,' she said, as kindly as she could. She did want to be kind to them all, when now, at last, she was able to think of them. She had time, facing eternity, to think of them. 'What can they matter, Cicely, the few things that belong to him. He has had life, which is greater than anything. It is his living quality that he has offered to you.'

'I know! I know!'

'And you know, Cicely . . .' she had to say it, to repeat it;

'there is still a chance. Valentine is full of hope.'

'I haven't much,' said the girl.

It made Catherine put her arm around her again as she had put it in the hotel bedroom. She had none herself. It brought them closer to him than either Valentine or Kathleen.

'Yet I do feel, strongly, that I ought to collect signatures as well as Kathleen.'

'If you feel so then you must.'

'Don't you feel that . . . that you ought to too?'

'What?' she asked, to gain time, 'collect signatures?' It was the test of her belief, her hope; and it amounted to nothing when she was asked directly. If they insisted, she would. She had no desire. And what was far more significant she had no false qualms of conscience about withholding herself. She stood on quite another plane. A plane where she had to preserve her soul for him. That was not her way of serving him. It meant no more to her, or to him, than going to visit him in the gaol. It did not matter to her if she never went to the gaol again. She would go. She would see him again. 'We shall see,' she answered.

And then Cicely did a thing that brought her into Christy's childhood. She went over to the corner where his rods and bats were piled and touched them with her hand. Catherine saw her as a vision of a little girl in a print dress, standing ghostlike on the playing field where the boy ran, fielding, his shirt open and his throat showing, the skin very brown against the white. His dark strong hair caught in the wind of his flight. He had said to her: I'm not a kissing sort. But he had kissed her all the same.

'They are funny, Cicely, when they are little boys, so terribly independent.'

'He must have been a darling.'

He had cried when the calf was killed in the butcher's. He had said: 'I am going to be a doctor and find out how to stop pain from happening.' 'They all were,' she answered.

'They are all so dark . . . but so different.'

'They were always different.' The difference had maintained itself. Cicely was coming towards her. She looked lost, forlorn. She had come back from the cricket-field but she was still a ghost. She had no right to be there. And then she saw that the girl was not really there, no more than she was herself. They were both the mere husks of themselves. She felt nothing perverse about it but at the same time she compelled her presence. She brought herself back:

'Cicely!' She wanted to get her out of Christy's room. 'If you like I will tell you about him . . . when he was a little boy. I will try to remember . . . Come up to my room.' She turned quickly from the girl's gratitude and led the way.

She made Cicely sit in the deep window-seat where they saw right across the park. The trees were beautiful to her, full of plumage. The gap was nearly filled where they had cut down the ash. Next year it wouldn't show at all.

'Last year,' she said, 'we burned cherry logs. Two old trees. They don't burn well. Christy and Valentine cut them.' She saw the saw, running smooth as silver, between them, and the red blood running out of the cherry-tree. The red, fresh wood of the tree. Christy and Valentine had wiped out their anger sawing the cherry-tree. They had come in with sweating bodies and a dark lively tenderness in their eyes.

'It was last winter that I met him,' Cicely said.

'Yes, I know.' He had told her. They had met at a meeting. They had walked in the rain. She had told him about her people.

'There was something about him . . . .'

She smiled, a little mocking smile. 'There is always something.' Cicely felt snubbed. She looked across the park as though she had not heard. There was a cloud like a fortress.

'He said the same thing to me: — there was something about her.'

And at once Cicely's face was lit. 'Did he?'

'Like all mothers I resented you.' Under ordinary circumstances she might have added that Cicely, in her turn would suffer the same resentment.

'But afterwards . . .'

She pretended not to hear. She was walking about her

room, touching things. To gain time. And then she forgot herself and found herself saying: 'They go from us. Another woman gets them. We have to accept it . . . .'

It made Cicely the rich one, the possessor. 'Oh,' she cried, and put out her hands.

Catherine would not look. She was away again, on the other side of the door which none of them had reached, and the boy was hers. Hers as he could never be this girl's or any other's. 'He was born on a stormy day, Cicely. The rain was coming down in torrents. Here, in this room.'

Cicely's hands lay limp in her lap. Her eyes had a sharp, greedy look in him.

Mitchell had taken Valentine out in the sailing boat, and she had been afraid for them. Christy had come easily, in the midst of her fear for Valentine. Her fear was so great that it had withheld her from the pain. But the after-birth had been terrible. She had nearly died. It was not until he was a few days old that she saw what he was like, a real son of Finn, red-haired. 'He had red hair.'

'Red hair!'

'Yes, and he kept it until he was three.' It was the winter that they had gone to Cathel St Denis that he had begun to darken. Even now, when you saw his hair through sunshine there were red gleams in it. They had been lost and she had gone down the Corniche road and met them, a group of other children round them listening to Kathleen (as she put it) telling poems. They had such pretty voices. People used to stop and listen, Kathleen particularly. She still had a lovely voice. 'He got lost once . . . in Salsburg, for a whole day. We found him in a police station, eating chocolate and weeping as though he had been sentenced to penal servitude.' He was in gaol. He was in gaol and they were going . . . . She said quickly: 'And after that we wrote his name and always his address on him somewhere and told him always to make for a policeman. He was always getting lost. He was nearly always in the moon and waking up and finding that he was not where all the others were.' What a lot of always. There was no need to speak in such a race. Cicely was staring at her.

'Didn't Valentine?'

'No. Valentine always knew where he was.'

'It seems strange to think of him as a little boy . . . and getting lost.'

It was strange to her to think of him as a young man, a young man who had made love to this girl. 'It will seem odd to you, Cicely, but it is easier to me to think of them all as little children.'

'I've heard that . . . that parents always think of them as never quite grown-up. He is very much grown-up . . . now.'

'Oh, he is quite grown up.'

It reached an impasse with Catherine. An extraordinary fatigue overcame her, drowsing her senses. She could go no further with it. She could not go on telling the girl details about him, feeding her with morsels of him out of her memory. That part of him was hers. What he had to give Cicely had not yet been given. She was there, on the rim of the well, looking, so far, down more upon her own image than upon his.

She looked past Cicely to the flowing heads of the trees. A wind had risen. They were going to have a storm. The clouds were massing before the wind, obscuring the blue sky. The wind was running through the trees like a river with a leaping movement. Some of the trees stood up to it like obstacles. She had not shown Cicely anything and she had scarcely told her anything. But the girl had not gone with Kathleen, so something had come of it. She heard herself saying: 'History was his strong point. He was always good on history.' All the heroes in turn — from William Tell to the Lord Mayor of Cork. Kathleen had said that somebody had said: a sow that eats her own farrow. The lapine that had eaten her young from fright. If they had to be destroyed they were better destroyed at birth. If they had to live for destruction then it was sheer instinct to let them live for as few hours as possible.

'He is splendid . . . .'

She saved herself from eulogy: 'He is the idealist of the family.'

'I know.'

But you can't know, she argued silently, you do not know the others. Cicely was sitting with her hands clasped round her knees and a stupid, rapt expression on her uplifted face. She was pretty in a gentle young way. She would not last. Catherine felt that she could no longer bear her. She put her hand on her shoulder. 'Now you must go. I must write to my cousin Mitchell before the post goes. When I have finished I shall come downstairs and we shall have tea.'

'Yes.' She got up, hesitated: 'I would like to look into Christy's room again . . . may I?'

'If you want to . . . .' She might have gone without asking, she thought. To have asked was a little too much.

When the door closed she sat down to think out a letter to Mitchell. She always thought out her letters to him, built them up for days beforehand. And she always read his letters to threads of meaning. It was queer how Mitchell's influence had lasted — outlasted so many other things. He had outlasted Luke. She had shared her childhood with Mitchell, her late childhood which is the most significant period in the making of consciousness. Early childhood was terribly over-rated. It was very important to parents, of course — a natural history lesson — and to those who developed neurosis. She had got nothing out of it except a haze in which certain records rang: a man saying tschaka! tschaka! to a donkey, or the fat woman going peepy behind a hedge, her drawers falling down like white plaster; or the eagle's wing that somebody brought in and spread out, showing the length and serration of the plumes. There was no significance in any of these things. They were exactly like dreaming that the photograph frame fell off the mantelshelf and was broken, and for the dream to come true — exactly as you had dreamed it. It was true, but of no importance. It proved nothing. It even meant nothing, no more than passing a mirror.

Mitchell began about the same time that she discovered that clean clothes made a difference; and coming home, found that home was home after absence, the parquet different from every other parquet. The portrait of the archbishop became hers as it had become the possession of other members of her family, by seeing it into a familiarity that did not make it necessary to see it.

Mitchell and a golden summer and a blaze of freesias. She had ridden his horse. They had read up in the Abbot's room. They had gone over to the Harps to stay and see a little cardboard play about a little Manchu princess who had been poisoned and died in agony without writhing or deranging her pillow or her coiffure. They had come back in the evening and walked between the shut marigold borders. Mitchell had never really gone away out of her early love for him. He had telegraphed that she was to write if there was hope and he sent his love. Her mind made the letter: I think they will hang him and Oh Mitchell, he is not ready. He does not know what a splendid moment it is and if he lives it will become ignominious, he will think as we all do that he has made a failure of everything; and now it is not that, and he is getting what he wanted, and I would give my life to save him but I cannot save him unless he is a little baby again and I can set him going differently. If she had the chance again she would never let him be born. It was worse for the others who were going to live. They would die in the end and the sum of their sufferings would be greater than his. She knew. It was like her feeling sorrier for Valentine in the courthouse than for Christy.

She began another letter telling him about the appeal and that Valentine would not believe that he was anything but innocent. And then, as always, she decided that she would write to Mitchell to-morrow. She would make up other letters to him through the rest of the day and the night, and to-morrow she would probably send him a few lines that left all the reading between them and which, being a man, would be lost to him. It made the correspondence quite safe. She liked to be safe with Mary because she liked her and they were friends. They saw all Mitchell's faults.

Cicely was waiting for her. She was wandering about the drawing-room with the listlessness of a moth. It made her say: 'Cicely dear, I'm sorry.'

'Oh! I don't mind . . . but the place is so full of him.'

It wasn't really any fuller of him than the rest of them. It was really emptier. She was thinking wrongly. But the child was so unhappy. 'It is indeed his home,' she said with emphatic gentleness, 'and it is a lovely home, don't you think?'

'It is a lovely place.'

'On the hill behind the orchards there is a view . . .' She regretted instantly. Kindness need not make her give away her treasures. She mastered the regret: 'We shall go out there presently and I will show you . . . one looks down into the valley.'

'To-morrow . . .' She wasn't thinking of Catherine's view. Her thoughts were rooted and their sway did not run, as Catherine's ran, beyond their limits. 'I am going to collect signatures.'

This time Catherine gave no support. 'You must realise, Cicely, that it would be better to go with somebody with your own, and Christy's, point of view, not to go with Kathleen. I think that Kathleen's canvassing will be confined to people who are likely to be of her own sort. I mean rather special, writing people. They are not like the rest of us.'

'I do realise . . . Kathleen is — rather special, isn't she?'

She was stupid, Catherine thought, nevertheless she answered with patience: 'She takes a lot of knowing.' She was a long way from knowing herself. She knew her, perhaps, instinctively. She knew where the fineness of her mind would establish her. It would take her out clear through every error. She would pay, of course, like the rest of the world. That was the difference between her and Christy, whose impulses were all impulses and would never suffer establishment. Life would have stopped the impulses . . . . She had a mother's pity for them all, and then was swept into futility the next moment. You could do nothing. There was a tealeaf floating in her cup. It began to whirl in the current where she had stirred her tea. Cicely hadn't touched the scones and she had scarcely eaten at lunch. 'You must eat, you know, if you are going to collect signatures. Nothing can be served by not eating. Eat, my poor child. You must keep yourself as strong as possible.'

Cicely took a scone. Far away Catherine heard the housebell ring and prayed to be preserved from visitors. Almost at the same instant Travers came towards her. 'There is a . . . a gentleman, ma'am.' She knew Travers' punctuation. 'He insists on seeing you.'

'What is his name?'

'He won't give it, ma'am.'

She wished Cicely wouldn't chew the morsel of scone as though it choked her. 'You can show him in here.' She did it to save her with Cicely. She knew that it was somebody who had come, namelessly, about Christy. She said so to Cicely who at once moved forward on her chair, with the greedy, bright look in her eyes.

He was a little man in grey flannel trousers and a pull-over and he came quickly towards her, the moment he saw her, as an arrow to a target. She stood up, up against him. Her height gave her an advantage. He stopped when she stood up, a little lost. He was quite young. He had fair hair and blue, small and troubled eyes. His mouth was very tightly shut, and when he opened it the words ran through quickly as pebbles through a sieve which holds back that which is too large. 'It's about Christy, ma'am, your son, they won't let any of us in to see him, at least none of us can go and we want you to give him a message. It is very urgent, very important. Tell him to take back pleading guilty. Tell him to say he never did it . . . .'

She interrupted him: 'Please! Please!' Don't make a play of it, her soul was pleading. Don't make tactics. It if it true it is true.

Cicely was saying in a clear newly responsible voice: 'I believe you know. He never did it. Who did it?'

He became slow, copying Cicely like a chameleon, responsible. 'How can we know which of us did it? We were all together.'

'Then why . . . ?' Catherine asked patiently. She had the dark glow of unity with Christy burning within her, enfolding him, saving him from all their foolishness and foolhardiness — and denials, and from their stupidities.

Her patience was only on the surface. If he was innocent then what were they doing? What did they mean? 'Then why . . . ?' she repeated without patience and with sharpness.

'Well, he was caught . . . he was the only one that was caught!'

'Yes,' said Catherine, carrying out the judgment, 'he was a fool to get caught!' She was so bitter against them. And when she turned and discovered another sort of judgment in Cicely's eyes — horror that she could, under the circumstances, call Christy a fool — she wanted to push them both out of the room. Yet she stood, the calmest of the three of them.

'There is no reason for my coming . . .' the young, nameless man was saying, 'except, except ma'am that I love that boy Christy, your son, ma'am ...'

'My son,' she said after him with something so deep in her low voice that they looked away from her. His love and Cicely's was remote to her, a drop in her own.

'There is no need for you to come,' said Cicely, her voice as sharp as Catherine's had been, 'on that score.'

'I think that you had really better come and see my other son, Christy's brother, about it. If there is anything . . . anything that you could do . . . he ought to know . . . .'

'Mr. Valentine? No. I don't think I can do that.' He looked at Cicely, making a chameleon of her. 'We can't. He's not on our side.'

'Christy would not want that.' Cicely made a summary of the man's notions to Catherine.

Catherine made a movement to go: 'Well then.' And then she thought of something and said it: 'Perhaps, Cicely, if he really means something, if he really can be of use, he will tell you? You are not in any way compelled to tell me.'

'I know.' Cicely put her hand out. 'Perhaps it is better . . . better that he should tell me.'

'Yes. Yes.' She went away from them with a sense of being a net in which they were trapped. Their fear was like the shyness of animals to her and as hopeless. No use showing them another way of life. She could stand in their place as well as her own. They could not stand in her's. They were deaf mutes about her. Yes. Yes. She went away from them. She went round the flower beds. The marguerites were beginning to take the place of the lilies. She preferred the marguerites. They had their eyes well open, but the lilies were dusty as death; they had the rot of death in their whiteness. Waxen body and waxen shroud. Oh! they were stupid those two! And yet they were lost, suffering without knowing where they were going to. It suffocated her. And for what? she asked, for what? Didn't they know? Was there really no glory in it . . . for Christy? It was that, the uncertainty. Where was she to place him — with the Jeanne d'Arcs or the unsure? When she was brought close to these, who loved him, she was shaken out of her communion with him. She could not allow that to happen. She must avoid; escape them, run away from them all. Her feet began to keep march with her thoughts. And then her thoughts went slower and she was walking quickly, almost running past the flowerbeds over the grass to the wall beyond the trees. She made direct for the gate where the wall needed mending. It took her through to the orchard where the apricot-trees were espaliered in the sunshine. She stood there, panting, glad that the fair young man had not seen her as she crossed the drive by the trees. He would have thought that she was lying in wait for him. Her heart battering against the hands she held pressed down on her breast. And always, she thought, this sunshine. This warm golden sunshine amidst the ripening fruit. She held her hands out in it, antagonistic, wishing that she could stop it . . . could stop the fruit from ripening . . . .

She was clear again in a moment, quieter, turning from her rebellion to find the orchard, as she always found it, beautiful with the laden trees and the shade lying in splashes under them. These trees had borne fruit before she had known life and would bear it after she ceased to know it through these mortal eyes. Yes. Yes. She could not stay now to look upon it. She wanted to be out on the hill beyond the orchard where, she had told Cicely the view was perfect. Perfect. Perfect. There were perfect things in the world but one ought never to say it. One ought to guard them in secret, never to let others see that one saw — like family love: there, and so profound that you had to hide it.

Ask him to take back pleading guilty! Could he not have said that before the sentence? Christy never took back anything. He held on to the end. Even in their childish maladies you never knew he was ill until he was so ill that you had to send for the doctor. You knew with the others: black circles under their eyes and droopiness and drowsiness and headaches or something, but with Christy never a sign. The throat specialist had said: 'He has a temperature that does not express disease.' It was not so much that he hid things but that he was withheld from them, in them, and not feeling them like other people as a disease. They consumed him and he never knew. In that he was on the Jeanne d'Arc side. Burning for causes . . . .

The air up here, where she had got above the hillside orchard, was always sharp as wind, straight from the sea. The sea was invisible. The range of purple hills with orange lights in them, and little white specks of houses was the country of her heart. Her spirit always rose up in this place Psyche-like above trifles. She had come so often. And to-day there were birds wheeling, blackened as she had dreamed of them. The birds were the only things out of her dream. The sky was a deep blue flocked by white masses of cloudy sheep and the silence had no terror in it. It was immense, and full of peace.

The young man was of no importance. It was odd, he trusted her and he would not trust Valentine. She was Christy's mother. Why should that, or anything, even Valentine's opposition, count now? She could not comprehend his distinctions. He loved Christy. Yet he could distinguish between Valentine and that girl, Cicely. Did he mean that they were not to tell Valentine but to tell Christy who could do nothing because he was shut in? She heard the orchard gate open behind her when she turned Cicely was there.

'I've been following you . . . I kept getting glimpses of you . . . .'

Oh, go back! Go back! her thoughts screamed, I don't want you.

'I'm so sorry,' Cicely was panting.

'But I didn't mean you to come . . . .' Catherine said softly.

'I know . . . but you said you wanted to show me the view . . . and I was so afraid that . . . that, Oh! the young man! . . . he wanted to tell me and he wouldn't tell you. He was so stupid . . . .'

'What did he tell you?' She did not want to know. It was insignificant to her and she wondered why her tongue asked the question.

'That's just it. He told me nothing — nothing that he hadn't told you, that we are to make Christy take back his plea. But it was different the way he implored me, begged me almost on his knees. He has convinced me that Valentine is right, that Christy is innocent . . . .'

Catherine watched the birds wheeling: 'Look. Look at those geese.'

Cicely looked: 'A flock of birds . . . Oh . . .' she turned to Catherine, '. . . Oh! if it should only be . . .'

Catherine stopped her in time. 'You must tell Christy when you see him, when you see him to-morrow with Kathleen.'

'But Kathleen . . .'

'Oh, my poor child, can you not remember that Kathleen, like you, would do anything to save him?' This caution! It separated those who said they loved him from themselves.

'I should like to be able to go now, to tell him at once.'

'Well . . . perhaps . . .'

Cicely could not wait: 'Perhaps . . . Oh could I, do you think?'

'Perhaps we could go in and if Valentine is there, or Redmond, they might be able to arrange it.'

They turned through the orchard again, descending into the laden trees on which the fruit hung in the sunlit air like Christmas decorations. The orchard was full of colour in the sunlight. They walked in silence. It was not until they were on the lawn again, where the flowerbeds close to the house that were cut into the turf looked minute in their trimness after the wild open hillside and the profuse orchard, that

Cicely said, with a strange lack of deliberateness that separated the words from the silence: 'I'd rather go in alone. I'll try to see Redmond.'

'If you wish. It might be better.' Catherine was relieved. She had been thinking what to do with the girl, what to say to her, and the idea of sitting beside her in the car nearly distracted her. She had had enough of her. And now, since the young man had so obviously given her a mission, given her hope she was no longer so necessary to her, or rather so on the verge of becoming necessary to her. Later, she might still be of use. 'Yes, it is better for you to see Redmond. He may be able to get you in to see Christy.'

'Oh! I hope so! I hope so! If I see Christy I shall tell him that I have been with you . . . Shall I give him a message, shall I . . ?'

'You may tell him that his mother's thoughts are continually with him.'

'And give him your love?'

'You need not do that.' She felt bitter, angry with her stupidity, when she said that.

Cicely was rebuked. Her own love made her clairvoyant. She felt the bitterness. 'I know I needn't . . . he has always been yours.'

And instantly Catherine was large again: 'Forgive me, Cicely.'

'Oh! There is nothing to forgive!'

And for a moment the old and the young woman stood close, linked into a sharp tenderness. Pity was in each of them. The moment fled and they were distinct again, emptied of sympathy, but comprehending each other.

The western sky was deepening over the park, pouring down a golden warmth and blackening the oak-trunks which stood out against it. It was the sunset of another day, Catherine thought. Day after day the sunset came, the night, the dawn. She had to count them now.

'Put your things on, Cicely. I will tell them that you are going.' On the steps she turned and took the girl in her arms: 'Do not mind me, poor child, if I seem cold . . . I am not cold.'

I know.' Cicely was ready to cry.

Catherine released her. 'There now. Be good, be brave. Do what you can.'

'I mean to do that . . . everything that is possible.'

'That is right.'

'And if I miss Valentine and you see him first . . . what will you tell him?'

'I shall tell him that, that you have now . . . come to his point of view.'

'Oh! You are . . .'

'And now, you will forgive me, I will say good-bye. You will be all right.'

She walked straight ahead, paying no attention to Cicely's 'I'll be quite all right.' At the foot of the staircase she felt Teazle at her skirt and sent him away. She did not look at the girl standing where she had left her, grazing after her with hurt, sullen eyes.

And the minute she heard the car buzz down the avenue she put on an old coat and went out of the house, out of the Gorabbey grounds, away from the fields that belonged to her, towards the mountains, walking quickly as though she, too, had found a sudden mission.

Chapter Two

Valentine came down late to breakfast. Catherine had already finished. She sent for fresh tea and waited. It was unlike her to idle in the morning.

'Didn't you sleep, Mother?'

'I slept extremely well.' She hadn't even dreamt.

Valentine regarded her. She looked as though she hadn't slept at all. 'Truth, Mother? . . . you aren't being . . . cynical.'

'Why should I? I tell you that I slept the moment my head touched the pillow.' She did not tell him that she had gone to bed at dawn. 'Did you see Cicely yesterday evening?'

'After I left her? No. I went down to Leix . . . to dinner. Bernard asked me. I telephoned during the afternoon,' he hesitated.

'And what is Bernard going to do?' Catherine asked after a pause.

'Anything and everything he can. He is doing it for Mitchell's sake. He said it — that he couldn't look Mitchell in the eyes if he didn't. He will never forgive Christy.'

Catherine was silent. This was the equivalent of the young man's fear to her. It gave her the same feeling. Bernard was looking at everything in the light of something that did not come near Christy. Christy was far away on a lonely road.

'I can't tell you, Mother, how often, only since yesterday morning, I've wished to God that Christy hadn't . . .'

'Don't . . . don't waste your time or thoughts,' she urged. She added, regarding him with quiet eyes, 'You know, Valentine, when there are two wheels, you see them in fairs, revolving in different directions, the outer one going at a much greater speed than the inner. I feel like that — that we are the inner wheel, going so slow and all the time against the speed of the other.' It was the nearest she could come to confession, to revelation of herself.

'But there is hope! There is truly every hope! And if Bernard adds his influence to the . . .'

'Influence!'

'Mother!' He was staring at her with widened, opened eyes. His hands were lying loosely on the table.

She evaded even an attempt at explanation, whirling him on to another idea: 'Cicely had a visitor yesterday, a young man who would not leave his name. Whatever he said to Cicely has convinced her that Christy never did it. She is entirely on your side.'

'There you are,' he exclaimed, greatly encouraged.

Catherine clasped her hands above her plate, she did not know what made her ask: 'When did you come in last night, Val? I didn't hear you.'

'I . . . I was awfully late . . .'

The way he fumbled over buttering his toast told her that he had stopped on the way, at Windyharbour. She tried to be fair to him. He had stopped, not meaning to stay perhaps. The girl had made him stay. It was such a little thing, to go to his girl, and so full of life. Life. The nights when she had lain awake tormenting herself over his sexual life with this unknown girl seemed very removed to her. It meant nothing to her now. It was as natural as his breathing. The vice had gone out of it. Pardon mounted in her, sublimating all that she had suffered because of him. She looked at him with strangely kind open eyes. He was a man and he had to run his man's life in his own way. She had every confidence in him. He was her son too . . .

But he was distant to her, closed up, like Kathleen. They had their own lives. Christy was folded back in her. She was heavy with Christy . . .

'You didn't hear me, did you?'

She answered: 'No, I didn't hear you.' She had come in after he had come in. She had come in with the dawn blazing in the sky, with the beginning day. She had been

sheltered in the dark moonless night and with the break of
day she had come in to bed, to sleep, to oblivion. The night
had been a sacrament to her, a communion with Christy.
She could not recover it now. It was stored in her — for
ever. 'I have decided, Valentine, to stay in town, in the hotel.'

'Are you sure you will like that? I mean, wouldn't it be
better to come back here, at least for the nights . . . .'

'No. No. It isn't practical, at all.'

'Righto.'

It was so clear to her that he didn't want her. 'It need
make no difference to your affairs. I shall, you see, find
more to do.'

'But will you? Are you going to collect too?'

She thought of saying: will it make any difference, but
said instead: 'we shall see,' and they looked at each other
with absorbed, questioning eyes. She had a sense of moving
in a dream, of unreality. At any moment Valentine would
turn into an object and the tea-pot would walk down the
table or become a mirror with a crowd passing through it.
The bridge on the willow-patterned plate and the lovelorn
Chinaman looping the loop under the willows into the sea
and eternity, into everlastingness . . . like Christy. Her body
felt too heavy a burden. She was ready to die, to die of
fatigue. She seized the tea-pot and poured out a cup of very
strong tea and drank it.

Valentine rose: 'I'm going at once. Where's Kathleen?
Are you coming with me?'

'Yes, I'll come with you. Kathleen did not come home last
night.'

'Kathleen . . . Mother . . .' His voice was full of
admiration. He fidgeted with his tie.

'Yes. Yes.' She knew what he meant, he admired
Kathleen. She had his own reserve. Christy was the
extrovert. 'She is a fund of strength.' Outwardly. What they
all were inwardly she dared not think. She only knew her
own madness. She was stronger now since she had taken
the tea, beginning to waken and not to see things far off, but
near; and very clear.

She dressed carefully. She wondered if she could take the

coat that she had worn during the night. It was crumpled and she had torn it. She gave it a good shaking, took the soiled handkerchiefs out of the pocket and decided that she would take it. If she were going to stay for several days it would be sure to come in useful. It was a brown tweed coat and she was very fond of it. She packed a few things quietly and without hurry. Valentine could wait a few minutes if she kept him. It could not make much difference. She descended the stairs with the valise in her hand. She had already told the servants that she was going to the hotel and to give her address to nobody. There was an impersonal quality about the hotel that had become natural to her. It was easier there than at home where everything made her think of Christy and his childhood and her own childhood. Valentine was sitting in a strangely bright blue car. He answered the surprise in her eyes:

'It's Bernard's. I came home in it last night.'

'It is a very gay tone of blue,' she said as she got in beside him. And as they sailed away down the avenue it struck her as quite part of the madness that they could go on saying ordinary things to each other, that there should seem nothing else to say. It made phrases like — it is a fine day, Mr Williams, seem real to her, and separated from an old man walking beside a row of asters. The torn brown coat was folded and on her knee. She held her doe-skin gauntletted hands clasped down on it. The corn was a day riper, and in one of the more distant fields they had begun to cut it. Yes. She would miss that if she stayed in town. It would be a mark less to her. 'I don't want to see them cutting the corn,' she said into Valentine's ear. They were approaching the village and as she spoke a file of children going to the chapel came in sight. It seemed in answer to her that Valentine blew the shrill cuckoo-horn of the car. All the children turned to look at them as they passed. When the road was empty again she said: 'How can Bernard tolerate a horn like that . . . I suppose it's Dicky.'

He laughed, a small blown-away mirthless laugh. 'Oh you may be sure Dicky chose it.'

Dicky was the same age as Christy. Until two years ago

they had been great friends. If Dicky had never gone to
Oxford they might still have been great friends and going
together and ... all this might never have happened. It had
happened. Dicky would be alive after the harvest. There
came over her a great wave of knowledge, as though it had
only just happened, that made her abruptly aware of the
truth. She had these spasms of becoming conscious of it all
anew as though in the intervals her spirit was able to
escape. As if the mere fact of breakfasting with Valentine
could take her into another world where one behaved
without suffering. She sat down very low in her place,
shrinking. They had begun to pass people. They were going
into town where there would be people in the streets,
occupied people, contained in their own important
trivialities. She would go to the hotel where they would
give her yet another bedroom, it was never the same one.
She would turn down the coverlet and put her nightdress
under the pillow, and let the water run from both taps and
wash her hands.

Valentine drove very fast through Windyharbour. There
was the cottage with the fuchsias falling over its brows, and
the villa farther on with the sunflowers and the little
banked lawn with steps in it. She always thought that very
pretty. Sometimes she saw a lady there with a tiny spaniel
walking down the tree steps or so into the little lawn —
Marie Antoinette through the wrong end of the opera
glasses . . . .

'Did you see that man?' Valentine asked. They were on
the edge of the town where the streets had taken on
continuity.

'Which man?' She had seen several at a corner.

'The one with the beard . . . with others, they were at the
corner.'

'No.' She had not distinguished a man with a beard from
the others.

'He's the ringleader . . . he's the murderer . . . Christy's
murderer . . . .'

'Oh don't!' she cried out, the car had swerved terribly.
'How can you know?'

Valentine did not answer. He was minding the traffic. They were going past a goods station and lorries were coming up in all directions. She was glad of the press of the traffic. It steadied him, and kept them from speaking until they arrived at the hotel.

Kathleen was standing, dressed for out-of-doors in the entrance hall. She turned as Catherine went towards her and saw her. Catherine could not help seeing the French stamp on the letter she held in her hand and the queer separated Russian-looking handwriting: Miss Kathleen Munster, Stacpoole Hotel . . . So she has her letters sent to the hotel, she thought, and felt nothing.

'I stayed the night here with Cicely.'

'With Cicely.'

'Yes, and Uncle Felix.' She gave a dry smile to Catherine. 'We are not so poisonous after all. He is a nice old man, and so sorry for Cicely.'

'Poor child.'

'Everybody,' said Kathleen, 'is sorry for Cicely.'

'There is no difficulty in understanding that,' Catherine said gravely, feeling that she had already said it a thousand times. One always felt sorry for defrauded love.

Kathleen put the letter into her handbag. And then she did a little thing that troubled Catherine. She took the letter out again, hesitated and put it suddenly back again, glancing at Catherine with a drained expression that convinced her that there was some reason, connected with the letter, why one should feel sorry for Kathleen too. 'Cicely came into Redmond's office last night in a great state. She is now convinced that Christy is going to get off. Some man has . . .'

'I know all about it,' Catherine interrupted.

'And you, Mother?'

She pretended not to hear.

'You have heard, Mother, but you do not want to answer.'

'Don't,' she pleaded. Kathleen was to much for her in this mood.

'I feel awful this morning, Mother, terrible, that it is all a dream, a nightmare. Nothing seems real, and the things . . .

the things that were so terribly real before now do not seem to count . . . I feel as if I can never care again . . . .'

A waiter was listening, and an old gentleman who was looking in a newspaper turned his ear towards them. Catherine drew her daughter away from them. She said nothing but she pressed Kathleen's arm.

'I could go out and shout it in the street. I have been doing that, for going round asking people you've never seen to sign . . . there's no difference . . . .'

'Have you . . .' asked Catherine, 'had much success?'

'Oh my dear Mother! Everybody signs. Nobody refuses. You should see the crowds pouring into Redmond's. He has had to engage two extra secretaries. I'm going to ask Valentine to let his clerks go round.'

The bitterness in her voice dropped like a plummet through her mood. Catherine was mute, helpless. And again everything dropped as from another plane and changed shape and meaning. She saw Valentine going away in the blue car behind the waiter who had been listening, and was now smiling broadly at some joke that had been made to him. She had the naked feeling that Kathleen meant when she talked about shouting in the street. A newsboy *was* shouting in the street, and God only knew what he was shouting. Kathleen was still wearing the dress that she had worn yesterday when she walked across the lawn to Teazle. Hours slipped through each other and night and day became one. Perhaps none of them had been to bed. She made a beckoning sign to the waiter, who came quickly, in little circumventing steps, round the chairs.

'Bring me a cocktail . . . a strong one,' she waved his attempted explanations away, 'I don't want any details.'

'I'll have a dry Martini,' Kathleen called after him.

'We must,' said Catherine with comfortless warning, 'take care . . . .'

'Oh I'll be all right directly . . . It's Cicely, Mother. She gets on my nerves. It would be easier, for us, if she weren't there, if Christy had never thought of wanting to marry her.'

They sat down by the curtained window. The newsboy was still shouting. The war touched Catherine in that moment as a force which could make women feel as she felt; the mothers of sons, of Christys. There had been wars and revolutions since the beginning of time. But the mothers were older. They had that much more wisdom. The mother of Cain must have known what it was.

'I don't know why any of us should want to marry.'

'But what an odd opinion, Kathy?' She finished her cocktail. She rarely called her Kathy. The boys did, but she herself could never do so without remembering Mitchell's good-bye when he went to China: So long, Cathy, and I'll come back to you, for you . . . .

'It will break us all up.'

They had been broken up for a long time, Catherine thought. And how queer that Kathleen did not realise it. Did it mean that she thought a great deal about them when she was away from them? Valentine was still at home but she felt that he was more parted from her than even Kathleen who had this craze for living abroad. 'We are already . . . broken up,' she said, thinking decisively of Valentine.

'I didn't mean that. I was thinking, on the contrary, that — this has united us, terribly.'

'I wasn't thinking of it either,' she said, feeling cryptic, and putting into her voice all that would not come clear in her speech. She felt joined to Kathleen subterraneously, hiddenly and in an indefinable way over the letter, and for the first time she connected Kathleen's war-work with her life. Kathleen came back into her life, and Valentine and Christy who had lived with her and quarrelled so continuously went into the distance. The days when Valentine and Christy had tormented her with their differences belonged to centuries ago. The quarrels were finished. Valentine was doing all that he could . . . he loved Christy and with a love that needed no declaration. It made her say: 'We can afford to give — everything to Cicely.'

'Everything!' Kathleen shrugged her shoulders mockingly.

'What is it, Kathleen?' She asked sympathetically and without curiosity.

'I'm . . . raw. Don't mind me. It will pass.'

Catherine regarded her. It was like getting to know a new person, not her daughter. They were all changing, foreign, deeper. But the roots of this had always been there. It became beautiful to her with its sorrow, plunging her into the seas in which she had passed the night. Great waves of sadness washed over her and she felt too strong and purified for tears or thoughts. There was only a great emptiness, a great nakedness as of a soul going bodiless to God. It was in this mood that she was of use to Christy, that she could hold him close — and safe.

'I think I'll have another Martini.'

Again she beckoned to the waiter.

'I . . . I feel stupid this morning . . . such a fool.'

Ah! Cleverness could drop away. The bright phrases. The mind could stop its gymnastics. Poor Kathy. It would pass. She would take up her writing again. She had preserved it from memories — not like the strawberry jam. It was different; Kathleen was a young woman. She would suffer many deaths. She was older, she was not like Kathleen. It was a true death to her. There'd be no more springtimes nor summers. The flowers would be paper flowers to her and the seas for ever going onwards . . . .

'Where is Cicely now?'

'She has gone with her uncle to Redmond's. They are dreadfully active. There are swarms of people round them.'

'Oh! I want to avoid that,' the protest slipped from her.

'I can't stand it either . . . and such people, Mother . . . all regarding him as a national hero. One woman congratulated me.'

Catherine's hands went rigid. To save herself she asked another question: 'Isn't Cicely going to see Christy this morning?'

'Yes. We have a rendez-vous here. She is coming here for me. I have promised to wait here. Redmond will bring her.'

Catherine looked up at the wall and saw an absurd touring picture, very blue and white, of the Bernese Oberland in an oblong frame. Oberland. Oblong. They were blind words to her. Her spirit widened out beyond them and her hands came loose again. She felt as though something had been born from her. 'I shall come with you.' Christy was cut off now from this world of passion, and passionate, mortal beliefs. It still surged and bubbled and people dipped their poor searching hands in it; unfriendly hands, many colours. Valentine had said (she had not noticed much at the time, but now she remembered it) that he was finished with politics. People were alike in spite of their beliefs, the same underneath . . . when you swung them out on the gallows tree. 'Yes. Yes. I wish to come. It is your turn, Kathy, and Cicely is going to see him. I know. But I shall come even if I can't see him. You can tell him that I have come.' It did not matter. She was the one amongst them that Christy would never doubt because she was his mother. Bone of her bone, flesh of her flesh.

'I must see him,' Kathleen said, as though she was going to be done out of it.

'You must.' Catherine said and reassured her. She felt a little deaf after her cocktail and there was a thrum like chloroform in her brain. It was in this thrum that she heard Kathleen's full name being called shrilly in a boy's voice. The name and the thrum thrummed together. She tried to control it but it went on and then she saw the boy coming towards them with a telegram. The effort at control eased into relief. The shouted name was actual and set her wits running amok on her. Kathleen was opening the telegram, and the boy with his ridiculous little drum-hat cocked on one side, was standing in official patience with one hand thrust into his breast pocket.

'There is no answer.' Kathleen tipped the boy and turned to her mother. 'It is . . . there is a man I know, in Paris. He is coming to see me . . . .'

'He is in love with you.'

'He has got leave. He is in the French Air Force . . . .'

She knew it was the man who had sent the letter. It was rather fine of him to come . . . if he knew. 'Does he know?'

'Yes.'

Now why, thought Catherine, isn't she glad? Kathleen was leaning forward with a defeated, listless air. The telegram was crumpled up in her hand. There was a reason. She wanted to lean forward to her and say: there are no reasons. Reasons do not count. The thrum was a little louder.

'Why,' Kathleen laid bare a history of resistance, 'does he come now?'

She was silent, mastering the thrum and, looking down the hall, she saw Cicely. Suddenly the buzz in her head stopped. She stood up, feeling quite clear and steady. Cicely had her back towards them. She was speaking to the man in the inquiry office. 'There's Cicely. She does not see us.'

They got up and went down the hall. When Cicely turned at Kathleen's touch on her sleeve Catherine noticed at once that her nose was shiny, and then that her voice was pitched in a higher key and time. She spoke quickly and in jerks as though she had been having a series of frights. She spoke to them just as if they had pounced out on her from behind a door.

'Oh! You here. I didn't see you.' And she fumbled over greeting Catherine.

Catherine re-adjusted her hat. She wanted to go right away with them to the gaol, but the way in which Cicely affected her made her say: 'I must just see my room. Won't you come up with me, Cicely? Don't you want to tidy . . .'

'No,' she answered abruptly, 'I'll do.'

Catherine did not make any further effort to see her room. Cicely had a note from Mr Redmond and they went straight to the gaol. The taxi was closed and Catherine kept her eyes shut until they arrived. She was forced to listen to Cicely's chatter. The girl was terribly excited this morning and absolutely convinced that Christy was going to be saved. When they got past the warder at the gate Catherine took her arm and said: 'Cicely dear, if I were you . . . I shouldn't be so certain before Christy.'

'But I want him to know, to feel . . .'

'Yes . . . but . . . you are not sure. None of us can be sure.'

'Oh!' cried the girl impatiently, 'you have no faith, you believe nothing . . .'

'It isn't what I believe, or do not believe, my poor child. It is what Christy believes.'

Cicely was arrested: 'You think it better for him not to believe that . . . that there is any hope?'

'Yes,' Catherine said it very deliberately, 'I do believe that.'

'Well!' said Kathleen in a gasp at her ear, 'I don't. I think Cicely is right. It is better for him to be full of hope until he is . . . until the last moment.'

Oh dear, Catherine thought, how stupid they are. Of course he will be full of hope until the last minute. Hope was the last thing to perish. She said oddly: 'But don't you see that we ought not to burden him with our hope . . . .'

Kathleen said quietly and comprehensively: 'I see.'

But Cicely walked on with a quick air of being in charge: 'I know that I shall not be able to hide it. I want him to know and feel that we are doing all that we can.' She went up to an official and gave him the letter that Redmond had written for her and Kathleen.

Catherine stood at the foot of the stone stairs and watched them go up. There was a strange sweet curve that had rested on her lips after she had reminded Kathleen to tell Christy that she had come, even if she could not see him. She saw the ladder in Cicely's stocking and the beauty of Kathleen's bare hand dropping against her dress. She continued to see Kathleen's hand for several minutes after she had turned the corner. She moved away from the stairs and began to walk up and down the passage.

These stone walls. These stone walls. Her hair was white at the temples. She had been young once like those two who had gone up the stairs. She had believed. She had gone through the Gulf Stream. She saw again a woman in Borneo with fine fringed filigree golden shields drooping from her ears and a baby at her breast. The woman's eyes had been drugged with peace. One could satisfy the body. The man with the silver buttons broke these images on her. He was asking her a question: what was she doing there?

'I am waiting for two ladies who have a permission to see a prisoner. He is in cell sixty-six.'

'That is a condemned cell. He is condemned . . . .'

'Yes. Yes,' she interrupted, dreading that he would ask her name, and break this unusual mercy of not knowing who it was. 'May I stay?' He was going to ask her name after all. It stiffened her manner, froze her against him: 'I only wish to know if I may wait here?'

'Yes. You may wait.' He froze too, and left her.

Far far away a whistle blew. Her steps seemed terribly loud on the flags. The present became more than present, fraught, loaded, heavy as stone in the prison silence, the chained silence. Her patience became as chains to her, a weariness. The knowledge of men, young men like her son, shut up in solitariness with thoughts that ought not to be indulged in, because they could not avoid, under the special circumstances, over indulgence struck her as deliberate madness. The whole psychology of civilisation went wrong on her. It exaggerated everything and in this exaggeration men got killed. Battles, revolutions, war and peace and politics were means to the end of life, to death. She felt grey as the walls about her. The waiting minutes lengthened. What were they telling him? His hair would be more crumpled than ever, and that smell was enough to give him a perpetual headache. Cicely would be clutching at him with all her over-strung and excited nerves. He would think of her all the day afterwards. She trusted Kathleen to encourage him, to give him true courage. She stopped once more at the stairs wishing she could go up and speak to him, open his locked door and take him up in her arms and run away with him as she had run with him out of the burning bedroom when the left wing of Gorabbey had taken fire. The slates had been red hot. She had walked up and down the lawn with the baby in her arms all the night, holding him close to warm him, and watching the firemen playing on the burning wing. Her father had died the winter afterwards, and the wing had never been properly rebuilt. They had simply roofed the lower storey that had been saved. The nurseries were there. When Valentine married the nurseries might be rebuilt and the bathroom put in. Christy belonged more to Gorabbey than any of them. They had moved in there after her father's death and

Christy had passed his childhood in the same places as her own had been passed. He had see-sawed on the same tree by the pond and fallen in and nearly drowned in the stems of the osiers. So had she.

Suddenly she saw the edge of Kathleen's skirt on the stairs. She looked up and saw that there were tears on the edge of her lowered eyes. She knew that Kathleen did not know that she was there so she said, softly: 'Well! and when Kathleen looked she looked away as though she did not see that she was crying.

Kathleen did not answer the 'well!' She came down and slipped her hand through Catherine's arm and together they walked down the passage, and turned at the end of it and walked back. In a moment or two she said: 'He seems very cheerful.'

'Is he?' Catherine could not be blinded.

'He does really seem to be quite cheerful.' She nearly said 'happy'.

'He has to appear like that,' Catherine said laconically.

'No. It isn't only appearance,' Kathleen affirmed, 'you feel that it is true . . . inside him.'

'I hope so.' She said it to support Kathleen. She was accepting no more judgements. Valentine had almost convinced her once. He had been false. It was enough for her.

'You cannot tell, Mother. You know he has done what he believed to be . . . heroic.' She remembered the woman who had congratulated her and in that moment forgave her.

'Yes. Yes.' There was no use in contradiction. 'I hope Cicely will not disturb this . . . this cheerfulness.'

'No. She was quite good. She is good for him . . . .'

'Yes, I suppose so.' It seemed very distant to her, Cicely's goodness for him. But Cicely was not distant. She was there when she turned.

She came straight up to Catherine and kissed her. 'He asked me to kiss you and . . .' She hesitated.

'Tell me exactly,' Catherine pleaded, interrupting her.

Cicely made an effort to get it 'exactly.' 'He said: tell Mother that I think . . . continually of her . . . continually.'

Ah. It was her own phrase, her own message matched back on her. It filled her and united her to him. The meaning was clear between them. A great trembling well of happiness ran through her and calmed her. It was meat for her day.

'He is delighted about the signatures, that they are pouring in, and all the propaganda . . . .' Cicely broke off, caught by the glint in Kathleen's eyes. 'It means something to him,' she added stubbornly.

'I know it does,' said Kathleen frankly, 'I am glad you told him. He ought to know. I suppose Redmond has already told him though.'

She knew that Valentine couldn't, for Valentine would not allow himself either to see or believe it. It had not occurred to her to tell him.

When they got outside Catherine was horrified to see a line of people, quite a procession, led by a man with a sandwich board on which, she had to stare at it fixedly before taking it in, was Christy's name. She shrank back as though to go through the gaol door again. Kathleen rescued her. 'Quick, Mother,' and again she put her arm through hers. Cicely had walked ahead, very erect. They caught up to her. At that moment a woman ran out of the little procession and came straight to Catherine. She was an old woman with a shawl pulled round her shoulders. She stood right in front of Catherine:

'You are his mother!'

It was anguish to Catherine. 'Yes, I am his mother.'

'Ah,' sighed the woman.

Catherine pushed her hands out, as though to push her away. She prayed to be deaf, not to hear what the woman would say. Her eyes met the eyes of the old woman. She was a very frail old woman and her eyes glistened with tears. It came quite clear to Catherine that she was face to face with her equal. Her spirit stood upright within her and gave mute secret greeting to this old unknown woman who knew her suffering; who understood.

'Ah. His mother . . . . May God help you!'

It was sincere. It seemed to pull Catherine before God. She took the woman's hands in hers, pressed them, and moved swiftly on. She felt as though she would choke. And what she wanted above everything was to get away, to get out of reach before somebody blew on a trumpet. She was terrified that they were going to make music somewhere out of that terrible line of people. She seemed to go through streets before they came up to her again, and Kathleen was flushed as though she had been quarrelling with Cicely. Catherine did not know for whom Cicely's 'I'm sorry' was meant or for what reason she said it. She again had that uncontrollable desire to escape from her. She looked at Kathleen with this desire loading her eyes in spite of herself. 'Please. I should like to go on alone?'

'Where, dear?'

Kathleen's gentleness was painful to her. There was suspicion in it. It braced her beyond the suspicion into proof that she knew what she was doing. 'If you don't mind,' she said coldly, 'I should like to speak to Redmond myself. I should like to know . . .'

'But you are going in the wrong direction,' Cicely said tactlessly.

She rebuked her with a glance, and turned. 'I know. I did not look where I was going. I only wanted to get away from those people.'

Cicely was no longer erect. She looked crumpled. She had an air that was more lost than Catherine's.

Kathleen did the right thing. She hailed a cab that was passing. 'You take it,' she said to Catherine, 'Cicely and I can walk.'

Cicely leaned in front of Kathleen to say: 'Are you going to collect after all?' There was a crusader-light in her eyes.

Catherine got in. She did not answer the question. She still had the feeling that she was running away from the people and that the trumpet was about to blow. Cicely was multiplied in her mind no matter where she looked, and she was terribly conscious of Kathleen's dark blue shoulder and the little coral rose with which she had pinned down a pleat in her dress. Her own voice sounded foreign to her as she said: 'Let us make no arrangement for lunch. I may take mine with Valentine.'

They both waved to her. She was suddenly aware that Cicely had changed her dress. She was in a green dress patterned with tiny daisy-like flowers. She was no longer like a fawn but like a field with daisies in it. Daisies on graves. In the green grass tiny, flushed flowers. The cab was passing the pastry shop where they always bought their cakes. Once again there would be people coming to tea and she would ask Valentine to order cakes ... people died after illness, after operations. It was not unusual. There was nothing unusual in it. Only if you died from illness it was because the body had had a shock, something had gone wrong and the body gave in. Your mind would not be prepared. It would be sudden enough to save your mind ...

The cab stopped. She sat on waiting for the cab to continue and when it did not she realised that this was Redmond's house. There was a crowd of children round the door and on the steps. She got out at once and paid the driver quickly and went through the children to the office door on which was printed 'Enter without knocking.' She asked the clerk if she could see Mr Redmond at once and alone? He returned immediately to say that she could.

She neither liked nor disliked this young man who had defended Christy so inadequately, but as he came forward to greet her she found herself comforted by him. 'I am glad that you are alone.'

'Everybody has gone ... they are making a demonstration.'

'I know ... unfortunately.'

He was puzzled, but diplomatic. He pushed out a chair for her.

She looked at him with candid interrogative eyes. 'I want you to tell me what you think? I am trusting you not to be led, or misled, by ...' she waved a hand in the direction of the window, 'all those people. I want your cold legal opinion, apart from all desire to draw any political omen. What do you think?'

He withdrew his eyes from her and began to fidget with a blotting roll on his desk. 'I have written to the Home Secretary ....'

She waited, giving him time, but as he waited too she

had to ask: 'What then?'

He looked up at her. He liked her. He had a feeling of great strength of spirit and courage in this silent, gentle-looking woman. But she distressed him. She denied him the mercy of all equivocation. 'Well, you know . . . it is a bad moment . . . .'

'On account of the war, you mean.' Nietzsche had said die at the right moment. And Christy wasn't ready. He wasn't ready. She realised that she was holding her hands so tight that they hurt. She realised too that he had stopped fidgeting and that his brows were unhappy. She felt sorry for him and said helping him out: 'It must be helpful . . . all that Valentine is doing . . . and my daughter too?'

His face cleared. 'We must bank on that, under the circumstances.'

This time she was silent.

'Of course, there is just a chance. Foch has begun to turn the luck. If the War look-out were less desperate, hopeless . . . you never can tell.'

She said abruptly: 'Thank you for being frank with me. I knew you would be.'

After a long moment he asked: 'And you?' What do you feel?'

He had no right to ask that. It shut her in again immediately, made her like ice to him. 'I can give you no legal opinion.'

'And a legal opinion,' he tried to console her, 'can only state what is . . . is there before one's eyes.'

'That was what I wanted.' A smile that looked as though it had travelled a long way came into her eyes. 'All those people. You are not blinded by them?'

'Not in the least,' he answered, and saw at once that she had trapped him.

'Nor am I.'

He tried to recover. 'But they are not to be ignored. They are doing something to public opinion.'

Public opinion repeated itself in her brain. His sentence would not be annulled by the public. 'What they are doing can have two effects,' she cleared his meaning for him, 'you know that as well as I do; for and against. There is the margin . . . but do not let us rely upon anything so changeable as a margin. This man, who spoke to my daughter, have you heard any more of him? Is he of any use?'

He shook his head. 'If one of them came forward and pleaded guilty instead . . .'

'If.' She smiled at him as she might have smiled at a child who wanted to live in the moon.

'I should like to be able to give you . . .'

She interrupted him, thrusting a hand out and taking the roller out of his reach. 'I want you to arrange for me to see my boy alone. Do not tell the others.'

'You have seen him?' he asked.

'Yesterday, not to-day, and not alone. I should like to see him . . .' she calculated secretly, 'alone and as soon as possible, as soon . . .'

'Why, of course . . .'

She ignored the interruption, 'as soon as possible after you have heard from the Home Secretary.'

He gave her a shrewd, rather hardish look. But he had nothing, he was assured, to fear from her. He promised and added: 'Valentine, I must tell you, is full of hope.'

It pricked her like the stab of an injection needle. Soon she would be completely inoculated. She had said it to Cicely. Kathleen had said it to her. They had said it to Christy. 'You see,' she separated everything from Valentine's 'hope,' 'we have not the, the doubtful comfort of sharing his views, Christy's views. We,' and again the long-travelling smile shone in her eyes, 'get nothing out of that. That is why there is nothing left to us but — the truth, the legal view.'

'The law sometimes changes its mind.'

She corrected him: 'The Home Secretary.'

He nodded and she rose. 'I am back at the hotel and I mean to stay there now until you let me know.'

He went with her to the door. He had a feeling that she was potent and that he was impotent. There was something about her that might work miracles and he had a wild notion of suggesting that she should try to see the Home Secretary herself. The lingering, obtuse smile in her eyes prevented him. He could not bear to rouse, in her, a hope that might fail. His arms hung loosely. Suddenly he asked: 'Have you seen the papers?'

The smile died. It went out like a spark. 'I have not read nor looked at a newspaper for weeks. I have avoided them. Do you think I can gain anything from reading any of them?'

Her bitterness filled him with pity. She was not so strong after all. 'No,' he admitted, 'forgive me.' He did not dare to read certain papers himself. Cuttings were always being sent to him anonymously. He did not want her to go. He felt useless to her, but in lingering he had a vague wish that she might do or say something that would show how he could help her. 'If there is anything that you think I ought to do,' he said stupidly. He was holding the door slightly open but not enough for her to pass through.

Poor young man. He had done so much and accomplished nothing. She could not tell him that it relieved her to be with him. It kept her mind quiet. With him she knew that they were in the grip of a power so strong that they had to be quiet. Her thoughts had to lie down in this place where there was only room for the bare truth. 'I feel safe with you,' she said, and he was rewarded. He was contented, unaware that she had revealed her own destitution. She desired that Christy should feel this safety . . . this absence of doubt. She stretched out her hand and pushed the door shut. 'I should like Christy to be preserved from all false expectations. Do you think that anything is to be gained for him by telling him about these demonstrations, these . . .' she searched for the word and did not find it, 'things in the newspapers. I would rather that he had the . . .' she searched again, 'peace of knowing only the bare truth. It's better for his soul. And his body . . .' She smiled again obscurely and the smile seemed to take, and hold, the rest of her meaning.

She radiated a mystic strength that confused him. He was holding the law out to her as one might hold out an addressed label to somebody who was already in the train. 'But if he likes to know?' he asked, remembering Christy's interest.

She wasn't believing that. 'He likes to know what we know.'

'Perhaps.'

'It isn't perhaps,' she denied, fighting for Christy's peace.

'But he does believe in why he did it,' he argued.

'He has got beyond that belief, by now.'

'How can you be sure?'

'I know my son,' she said quietly. It was not really that she knew him but that in the secret agonies that she had endured for him she had acquired a profound and ineradicable sense of feeling for him. She knew what he needed as though he were unborn to her and dependent upon her streams. She said abruptly: 'Do you believe in prayer?'

Edward Redmond went red up to his ears: 'Why! of course!' he stammered.

She put her hand on his arm. 'There is no of course about that either.' She had frightened him, turned evangelist upon his sincere limitations. And he had done more for her than he thought, for he had shown her a futility that was utterly safe to her. She could go out of this room now into — liberty. There was nothing between her and Christy. There was only that region wherein the spirit of each of them knew God and touched. Coming down at daybreak from the mountains she had seen a doe rise from sleep. It took shape at first like a shadow from the scattering night and then, moulded against the East, became warm and living and strangely lovely. It was a drop of beauty, liquid as a jewel in the morning darkness. The light was made to show through it in order to show it. She thought of the doe, looking in Redmond's shy eyes and asking him if he believed in prayer. 'And in miracles?'

He was not so certain: 'Sometimes.'

Poor young man. He had been like a rock of truth to her, of sense; and now she was springing roses upon him. 'In France,' she said, 'they have made roses spring from rocks.'

He gave a queer little amorphous laugh that convinced

her that he thought she was mad. She said good-bye to him and went out, holding her head like a queen and moving with an air that cut the youngsters on the doorstep in two as neatly as a blade.

She went back to the hotel hoping that Kathleen would come in soon for she could not face lunching in the hotel dining-room, and the thought of a tray in her bedroom made her feel that she would rather go without. The problem was solved by Valentine who was awaiting her.

'Have you seen the midday *Times*?'

She shook her head. She wanted to beg him not to tell her what it was, and then she saw a foreign looking man in a strange uniform pacing up and down in the lounge and she thought of Kathleen's telegram.

'This is Bernard's doing . . .' Valentine shook a hand into a newspaper. 'This is splendid of him. He's on the Board of Directors.'

'What board?'

'The *Times* . . . .'

'Don't,' she cried out at last, 'don't, I beg you. I don't want to hear it.' Her voice and eyes were distraught. He opened up all that had been closed so completely in Redmond's office. When she thought of it, that office had been a refuge to her.

The excitement abated in Valentine. He folded up the paper and put it in his pocket. He saw at once that it meant nothing to her and he accepted it, although it, apparently, meant a great deal to him. 'Lunch, I suppose?'

'Wherever you choose, Valentine, as long as I can share it with you.'

His eyes softened and he took her arm. 'I prefer Sheerey's. We can have a screened-in table.'

She hesitated, again looking at the stranger: 'I'm puzzled about that man.' She felt she was being childish. 'Kathleen is expecting a friend.'

He pressed her forward with him towards the door. 'Well, we can't go up and ask him if he belongs to Kathleen. Kathleen ought to be here to pick up her own men.' She was silent and he asked when they got out into the street: 'Have you seen Christy?'

She told him that she hadn't but that she had gone to the gaol with the others.

'I should like him to see this . . . .'

She wheeled round on him: 'but if it is Bernard's doing!'

He cried back on her: 'But if it is going to get him off!'

Oh, my God! she prayed, keep me from going mad, keep me clear. She thought desperately for Christy. Redmond had said: 'he does believe in why he did it.' If he still believed then Bernard's redemption would be treachery to him. And if he had truly got beyond that belief — if he was where he and she stood together and were strong — then all that Bernard or anybody might do counted for nothing. 'It is so hard to be sure of what will please Christy,' she said in low desperate tones, 'and if I were you, Valentine, I should . . . I should do everything, as you are, but I should tell him nothing. It will only confuse him.'

'Confuse him!' he laughed.

His laugh gave her his full mind with his politics and his love for his brother mixed up and streaked with each other, bitter . . . and true.

'Confuse!' he repeated.

She thought out to him wildly: 'Don't! It was not Christy, it could not be Christy. Christy was amongst the young men of the day who were beyond the confusion, who were giving their lives in a terror that was beyond confusion. He knew what he was doing. It was the only thing that she was certain about concerning him. And it was the only thing that ever made her think hardly of him. He was leaving the terror, the desolation, to the others who would have long, lonely, ashy years in which to comprehend it. This was the root of her feeling for Cicely. 'How,' she asked, 'are you going to tell Cicely about this, this in the *Times*?' It would send her in hot anger to Bernard. The confusion really swelled in her then and, for a moment, she slipped and felt her wits sinking into it. She gripped Valentine's arm.

'It won't be necessary to tell her.'

'I hope she won't see it. Oh, Valentine, couldn't we get hold of her in time?'

The bitterness went out of him and for a second he was

dark to her but when his voice came it was full of feeling:
'There, Mother, don't let it worry you. I'll explain it to her.
After all she's his girl. You can trust her to prefer him alive . . . .'

She stopped him. That trust was their level. 'I know. I
know.'

'If she isn't large enough . . .' he began with the bitterness
back in his voice.

'Of course she is large enough,' she interrupted him
again, and she added with something of his own inflection:
'aren't we all . . . large enough.' She felt drab, disturbed,
muddied as any of them and no safer. The security of the
extremes to which Redmond had plunged her was no
longer hers. Now that they had begun to discuss these
details with each other it seemed to her that centuries had
passed through her since she had listened to Christy's
sentence and since they had been *unable* to talk about it.
Now they were talking and the talk was terrible to her,
comfortless. What could it matter if Bernard, simply
because he could not 'look Mitchell in the eyes' if he didn't,
had got some sort of apology for Christy into the *Times*.
What did it matter if Cicely's anger would be certain and
Christy's uncertain because none of them might tell him.
And suddenly, there, walking into Sheerey's with her arm
so agedly in Valentine's, she suffered a piercing desire to
see Christy, to touch him, to reach him to the depths. Ah.
Even faith could cheat her and the silent realm of the spirit
cry out for wings to beat in it!

'Now,' said Valentine at her ear, 'for a quiet corner . . .
one of those tables by the screens.'

She saw the round fluting of the wooden screen and the
sharp pointed fingers of the palms above it. The coldness of
the grave came over her and she shivered. Meanings,
political and spiritual and emotional, fell down upon her
like icicles, strong enough to withstand the sunlight. 'I am
so cold.' She meant that her soul was cold and beyond
deliverance. She heard Valentine order two cocktails
without asking her. 'I wonder,' she said, 'if I may take off
my hat.'

'Take it off. Take it off,' he answered, and leaned over

and helped her. He hung it up on the peg beside his own, patted down the flaps of his dark blue pockets, felt for the newspaper, took it out, glanced at it and put it back again.

'Do read it, if you want to. Only don't read it to me. I can imagine it.'

He looked at her with an expression that conveyed clearly that he did not think that it was the right moment to rely upon the imagination.

'I have already read it.'

'I know, but you want to read it again.' She did not feel perverse or against him, only that she had to pull his desire through for him. The cocktails came. He drank his at one gulp, 'take that' and he gave her hers, 'you need it,' and he produced the paper again and began to read it. The waiter gave her the menu. It was a piece of white pasteboard to her with coloured nasturtiums in the corner and a falling spray of leaves that descended to the entremets. The waiter's thumb had an enormous cushion. The Mount of Venus. Travels were marked there and the length of life. A palmist had told her that she was going to have a long life, a long life and a very happy one. She drank. Palmistry was one of the booths of life. You looked in and saw yourself concave or convex, as you might be or never could be.

'Order something, Mother.'

Again she saw the waiter's hand, the fingers spread this time, a peculiar male gentleness in the lightness of his touch. She did not want to order anything. Her will was paradised. She took the menu and handed it to her son. 'You do it . . . I can't.' The waiter was hovering over them like a crow, like a gigantic magpie.

She ate what came. Valentine was merciful and did not again speak of Bernard. She had sometimes thought, and Bernard had hoped, that Valentine would marry one of Bernard's girls. Ellen, perhaps. She was the least ugly. They were all so clever that you forgot the ugliness. If they had been pretty — like Cicely — you would have hated the cleverness. It would have been too much. There had to be a limit to the gifts one could bear, particularly in a woman. 'Yesterday . . . did you see Ellen?'

'Nelly. Yes, she was there. She . . . .'

'She was sorry . . . ?' she hardly knew what she wanted to ask. She was asking instinctively as though, again, she wanted to pull something through for him.

'She wasn't. She was worse than Bernard . . . against Christy.'

'Yes. You knew that. But she was sorry . . . for you.'

'I don't know what she was for me,' he said, and put a forkful of salad into his mouth.

'You mean . . .' she felt as clever as Ellen, 'that she wasn't — large.'

'I don't know what I mean, what you mean,' he answered, and she felt that Ellen had destroyed something in him.

'You must take a lot for granted.'

'I do. But, you will confess, there is a limit.'

If he could still make limits with her then he hadn't got very far with Ellen. She neither knew the name or the creed of the girl in Windyharbour, but she was confirmed, in that moment of Ellen's destroying, that she had no limits. She was silent. She had finished eating and she sat with her hands folded, patient and, in spite of the cocktail, thoughtless. Presently he asked if she would have coffee. She said no at first, and then quickly: 'Yes, but let us go back to the hotel for it. I am anxious about that young man.'

'How strange of you.'

The warm kindness in his teasing voice almost made her tell him about Kathleen. It was Kathleen that she was anxious about. 'It isn't strange . . .'

'No?' he shrugged his shoulders, and she was aware that his thoughts were absent. He was not thinking either of her or of the strange young man. He took a cigarette out of his case, tapping it in an odd way that reminded her sharply of Christy saying — badly made cigarettes. Christy went in for native manufacture. It had been quite a hardship in the house always having to make certain of trade-marks in order to avoid argument. A triviality like argument . . .

They walked back slowly to the hotel and found Kathleen and Cicely and the stranger all in the lounge on the same chesterfield, and all speaking French. The young man's name was André Grenier. He and Valentine began talking war experiences at once, and with an ease on Valentine's part that revealed to her that it was not unusual for him to speak of the war. The atmosphere of Gorabbey became unreal to her, muted as family bodies in a vault, merged in their differences. Death — and no dispute. Valentine had been home for nearly two years and his wound still reminded them of his absence occasionally. But only occasionally. She had had no fears for him, none. And she had been right. He was here now as proof of the soundness of her instincts. Time had flown. She tried, for one flying second, to imagine two years ahead and chased the image away and made herself listen. The young man was only a temporary soldier. He had, Kathleen was explaining, written books and was going to write more. Ah. That explained everything. It did not explain Kathleen's despair because he was coming to see her. He was in Kathleen's world. It drew and repelled her. She always felt a little chilly amongst clever people, as though their cleverness was an extra garment that preserved them from the weather of current ideas. They were able to deal with them whereas her place was at home, by the fireside, in Gorabbey — where, it was now evident, they had a justice and a peace that was not to be found elsewhere.

She studied this André Grenier. He had an air of race like a Roman and was too good-looking to deserve brains. She was struck suddenly by his resemblance to Kathleen. If they married they would be taken for brother and sister, and people would say that they had grown to be like each other. There was no growth about it. They were like each other. Looking from him to Kathleen she became clairvoyantly conscious of the passion between them. There shone in each of them a dark glow that was made almost incestuous by their resemblance. There was something wrong about it, something dark — and holy. Abelard and Heloise. She saw instantly a field white with milfoil in St Gildas and the current that made their sails powerless in the Morbihan. The still magic air and suffocating skies that fostered passion. No love had ever been generated there to be forgotten. It lived on and on and was a station for the footsteps of lovers. It was terrible and strong, so strong that it burnt up all impurities, all infidelities. She was caught by the turn of Cicely's head, a defensive gesture as though she were being challenged by Valentine. What now? But he was only asking where she had learned to speak French.

'I was sent to a convent in Flanders. I was there for two years.'

Flanders had another association at the moment, into which Cicely, by having gone to a convent there, was newly brought. It tempered her a little, she could see, to Valentine. Cicely was very animated when she talked to André Grenier. Kathleen noticed it and it brought a subdued smile into her eyes, tolerant, and then turning to sadness. She wanted to console her, to tell her that it (she really did not know what) was a little thing and would come right. And then she wondered what were André Grenier's views, and suddenly gathered them from what he was saying to Cicely who had said something to him that had given him a clue.

'In France we know what revolution is.'

'Exactly.' She seemed to claim him with the word.

But Kathleen took possession. 'Don't be cynical, Dédé. This poor girl is an idealist. And this . . .' she shook her head at him, 'is not the moment.'

He had a delightful laugh with a note in it of some animal in love.

No. It was not the moment. She thought of Christy in his evil smelling cell. It was his moment . . . and he was not ready. He was their centre and he was absent. There thoughts shone from him as rays and there was no return. She felt in that instant that there could be no return, no reflection . . .

Valentine was standing beside the Frenchman, very quiet and thoughtful, saying nothing, and looking very like a lean older brother. His reserve gave Catherine a spark of satisfaction. He shot her a serious glance and suddenly said that he was going. Cicely stood up and said that she would like to go too, to go with him, if he didn't mind. He looked relieved. Catherine knew what they would talk about and was indifferent. The indifference was like sleep to her. She shook herself out of it as they disappeared, and it was like shaking herself out of a dream into the reality of other people — into Kathleen and this young man. On the couch where Cicely had been sitting was a French book. She reached for it and opened it. It was a book on religion, on the rebirth of faith in France. She looked from it sharply to André Grenier.

'It was written by a friend of mine. He was killed two months ago.'

'The last time I saw him,' Kathleen said, 'he was eating mussels.'

'It consists of letters to his friends.'

'Including you?' Catherine asked.

'Including me.'

'And did you write to him . . . on the same subject?' she had no desire to be inquisitive.

'He was too earnest to convince one,' Kathleen said.

'Yes,' he answered, 'I gave him letter for letter.'

'You were against him?'

Again he laughed and she was warmed as by a living warmth as he said: 'No . . . not exactly.'

'He is not earnest, mother, not like Jules was . . .'

He interrupted her: 'But yes, Katrine, I am, you know quite well that I am, but not in that way. He was rare, Madame, in his point of view, solitary. He believed in miracles . . .'

'So do I.' She put an end to even the pretence of levity. Something was scraped bare between her and this warm-laughtered man. It was as though they leaned out of the same window and saw the same growths, or as if long ago they had sat at Jerome's knees touching the skirts of the truthseeker. Their beings had known identical revelations even if they had received them in different ways and in different ages.

'But you cannot . . .' said Kathleen slowly, 'expect miracles to happen . . . to happen when we want them.' Her voice became abruptly bitter with unbelief: 'They never happen.'

Catherine moved to the chesterfield beside her, but she did not touch her. She opened the book, turned the pages idly and shut it again. Her mind was again in Redmond's office, confronting that young man. The same clearance of soul, but for a different reason, came over her. Here, she thought, is the rock and the roses and she said, meeting Grenier's dark burning eyes: 'In France you have had roses spring from rocks . . . the roses come out of your hearts.' She had a sense of saying something to him that he would never suffer to be forgotten, and then her thoughts saw the queen of Hungary with her dress full of roses and the fishes rising out of the lake to Francis. It was some rhythm of the spirit, childlike and unstained by experience. 'It is experience that kills . . . .'

'The slow stain of life . . .' Kathleen quoted mockingly.

Catherine dreaded that Grenier would say something clever, but he was silent, and his eyes were gentle in their ardour, full of acknowledgment. The threads went to and from between them without breaking, and something was made for them in eternity.

'The only thing,' Kathleen remarked, with an air of keeping the conversation going, 'is to look at life scientifically . . . like William James,' she tossed the phrase to Grenier like a challenge which revealed to Catherine that it was a familiar battle-ground.

But all he said was: 'The life we make . . . there is a life that is made for us.'

'A preservation,' Catherine said very quickly, afraid that he was going to snap the threads by saying something else.

Kathleen snapped in like a pair of scissors: 'Nothing is a preservation. Nothing. We are exposed from the beginning. It is only when we know how to deal with it. Take a cigarette.' She held the red Russian cigarette case out to Grenier.

Catherine thought: she doesn't want him to be sympathetic. She is against him. Perhaps they had quarrelled. She put the book back on the chesterfield and got up.

'Don't go, Mother, please.'

'But you don't want me?'

'Don't go. Won't you have some coffee?'

She had forgotten the coffee. She didn't want it, it was an excuse. 'Yes, I'll have some coffee.' She never knew what made her say to Grenier, 'I came here, to the hotel, to escape from visitors. I have been avoiding people . . . for days.'

'And you find me here!' he laughed.

'You do not seem like a visitor.'

'Oh, but he is! He is going away again in a few hours,' Kathleen said sharply.

'Then you must have a great deal to say to each other.'

'No. It has all been said. Hasn't it, Dédé . . . over and over?'

'I don't know.' He gave Catherine her cup of coffee from the tray.

She took it from him thinking that she had told Travers to give nobody her address and that Kathleen had given him the address of the hotel and how she did not mind meeting him because he was a complete stranger to her. And looking down the lounge she saw the waiter coming back to them with a card on a tray: 'There!' she exclaimed, 'I am sure somebody has found me. It was fatal to say that I had escaped.'

Kathleen took the card. 'It's Jenny Lysaght . . . .'

Catherine rose. 'I shall take her up to my room. She . . . Bernard . . . have you seen the midday *Times*? Bernard has . . . Valentine told me, been splendid. No . . .' to Grenier, 'I am not going to say good-bye. I am going to see you again.'

Jenny Lysaght kissed her. 'I went out to Gorabbey this morning. I wasn't at home when Valentine came. Dickey's had a fracture, nothing serious, and then I went to the Sheridan where you always stay . . .'

'I have been staying here,' Catherine explained, 'to get away from people.'

'I know.'

It reminded her of Cicely. It was her regular phrase. But Jenny really did know. She was a kind and truly sympathetic woman and full of sense. She said as she shut the bedroom door: 'You do know, Jenny.'

'My dear, my heart aches for you.'

'I'm sorry that I did not tell Valentine to explain that I . . . I didn't know that he was going out to you . . .'

'And I wasn't there. Nelly told me, and Bernard, and I went out at once, this morning after I got back. When you weren't at the Sheridan I went to Valentine's place but he had just gone out to lunch, nobody knew where.'

It was like a lot of little waves coming in. You had to count for the seventh. Every seventh wave she might say something that mattered. She couldn't bear to count. She said directly, breaking the suspense: 'Bernard has been very kind. Everybody is doing what is possible, but, you will understand, Jenny, I believe in nothing . . . .'

'I know.'

'I did not feel like this when Valentine was away.'

'And I did. I knew that Terry would never come back.'

They looked at each other with the comprehension of women who have had the same pains and agonies, who were the same age, and who knew everything.

'Bernard has set certain wires working.'

'Valentine is very pleased.'

Out of the pause Jenny Lysaght moved on to another branch. 'Nelly was truly distressed. She felt that she had not been kind . . . kind enough. She has a heart of gold underneath all those brains of hers.'

'They are so clever, these children of ours, Jenny!'

'We ought to be proud of them.'

'Are we not?'

'I often wish my girls were fools and ever so pretty. Yours, Katey, are both clever and good looking.'

She hated being called Katey, but Jenny always did it. She ended all her own family with an ell wy. She had even tried to call Valentine Valley, but he had rebelled against it. There was another pause. Jenny looked on the verge of explaining something, but held it back. She was practical instead.

'What are you going to do this afternoon?'

Catherine was truthful. 'I don't know. I honestly don't know what to do with myself.' Cicely had gone away with Valentine and Kathleen belonged to André Grenier's few hours. She was in Jenny Lysaght's power.

'Dickey has asked me to see about his foxhound, Bluebell, she's with the vet. Will you come?'

She had to repeat it to herself to make quite certain that she was being invited to visit Dicky's hound at the vet's. Only Jenny could have suggested it.

'She's with Mason in Anselm Street. She's going to have puppies.'

They always had Mason when anything went wrong with the horses. 'Oh,' she said stupidly, 'do you think I can?'S

'Come,' said Jenny, beginning to put on the gloves that she had been holding in her hands. 'We'll walk. I must walk more. I'm getting too fat to be comfortable. Bernard, on the contrary, is getting far too thin.' She added, connecting her unspoken thoughts, 'We are going to Vichy.'

Catherine went to the basin and turned on the hot water. She began to wash her hands. She twisted her hands over and over in a thick lather and let it run off under the running tap. Acutely and for no reason she saw the sanitary pan in Christy's cell and felt the smell. 'Have you ever been inside a gaol, Jenny?'

'No.'

'Well, you ought to go. It's more deserving than half your committees.'

There was a pained, perplexed look on Jenny's face, but she went on buttoning her gloves.

'It makes me feel that I am losing my reason and . . . this, this going to the vet's to see Dicky's Bluebell . . .' she turned off the water. The water and her voice stopped together. In quite another voice, lower and quite normal, she said: 'but of course I shall go. It is the best thing to do. How old is Bluebell?'

'She's three. This is her first litter.'

Teazle was four. Christy had brought him home in his pocket and put him on the library table and he had lapped up all the ink before they could stop him, and sprawled with his helpless legs and ink-dripping tongue over a packet of newly addressed envelopes. Christy had said: 'He is nearly as clumsy as me . . . .'

'I've got to ask Mason to register them at the Kennel club.'

'And have them photographed?'

Jenny took her seriously: 'Why, of course. Dicky is awfully particular.'

She cried out then: 'Oh! Don't ask me. I can't.' She thought furiously of an excuse and invented one: 'I must buy sheets. All our sheets are going to pieces at once. They're wedding ones. You'd think they'd been timed to a second.'

Jenny saved her, pretending not to hear: 'Bernard said I was to tell you he would like to see you but he is very busy just now. He will do everything he can and is already doing all that he thinks can be of use. He doesn't approve of Redmond, and thinks it was a mistake to have chosen any but a conservative. But you did it for the best.'

'Valentine chose him. He considered it wiser to have a man from that side.'

'I am surprised at Bernard taking it up after Redmond had had his finger in it. It shows how much he cares.'

'He cares very much for Mitchell,' she said coldly. It had become artificial to her, paint on Jenny's true sincerity. The woman in the street who had asked God to help her had come closer to her. And she had known Jenny before she married Bernard. Their children had spent intimate summers together. She did not want to go with her to the vet's. Neither did she want to buy sheets, nor did she want to be alone.

'He cares very much for you all as you know quite well, but you cannot on that account expect him to change his principles.'

Principles and cardinal virtues and the four points of the compass tumbled on top of her.

'He was terribly shaken, Katey . . . .'

There! They were real. They were true. They could afford to say the truth to her. But she was in a realm beyond their reach. She was shut in with Christy on the other side of the thunderstorm. It made her look at Jenny as though the pity and consolation were on her side. Jenny had nothing to give her; nothing that she could take.

'Do not mind me, Jenny. I am not ungrateful. I just do not feel.'

'I know. I really do know. That is why I think you had better come with me . . . to Mason's, or to buy sheets, if you want to. I'm the right sort of woman for you to be with. Come.'

There was no denying her. Obediently, hypnotised by Jenny's stronger will and dread of a drifting afternoon, she went with her.

Kathleen was no longer in the lounge when she went out. She cast one searching glance for her and as she did not see her, said nothing. She chose the vet's rather than the sheets. It left the talking to Jenny. They went from there to the Kennel Club, and then Jenny took her to see a woman whose husband had been drowned and who was destitute and living in a room in a slummy crowded street. Jenny had found work for her in one of Bernard's mills. They did not once speak of Christy. Jenny brought her back to the hotel before dinner and would not come in as she was anxious to get back in time to dine with Bernard.

It seemed to Catherine that she was no sooner inside the vestibule door than Cicely rushed out upon her.

'Where have you been? Oh, I thought you were never going to come back! Have you been with Christy?'

'No,' she said coldly, and looking round to make sure that nobody was noticing the excited girl, 'no. I am very tired, Cicely. Let us go up to my room.' She led the way to the lift. She shut the door of the bedroom herself and followed Cicely round the bed. 'I have been out. I've been to see a vet with Lady Lysaght.'

'To a vet's!'

The absurd horror on the child's face annoyed her. 'Not for myself, of course.'

'But . . . how could you?'

The judgement startled her like an accident, a trifling thing like touching a dish and finding it burning hot when you thought it was cold. She dropped the dish. 'Oh . . . what is the matter, Cicely, what is wrong?' It was only then that she saw the sheaf of papers in the girl's hands.

'Did you see the *Times* . . . do you know about it?' She was not asking questions but demanding explanations.

'No, I did not see it. Bernard told me.'

'Bernard did it?'

'Did what?'

'Oh please! Please! Don't fence with me. Be honest!'

The dish was no longer hot to her. 'My poor child. What is it? It is you who must be honest with me.' And for an everlasting second she thought that Redmond had broken his word to her and that the papers had published some terrible decision. She ought to have asked if there was a message before she came up. 'What is it?'

Cicely was twisting the papers, moaning: 'Oh now! . . . between them . . . between them what are they going to do . . . Oh Christy!' She flung suddenly at Catherine: 'They have betrayed him.'

It was like being hit with a stone. His friends could not betray him. The girl was demented. She had misconstrued what Valentine had thought was going to get him off. 'Nonsense, Cicely, his own brother could not betray him . . .'

'But between them!' she screamed.

The word betrayal covered Catherine's senses with black wings. It spread and hovered. From under it she asked: 'Between who? Oh my dear, do you not see that I do not know what you are talking about.'

Cicely thrust the papers at her. She saw that they were mostly typewritten and there was a small closely printed sheet.

'Read! Read!'

She thrust them back on her. 'Do not ask me.' They were like two people on a narrow bridge, neither of them would go back. Catherine pushed past her. 'If you cannot tell me what has happened then go, I beg you to go . . . out of the room.'

Cicely's hysteria was arrested: 'It's the others now. Now they say that he must have been a spy or the *Times* would not stand up for him. They are not going to help him any more. They . . . they are against him . . . they have given him up!'

Black wings were joined to black wings. Beneath them Christy swung, forward and back, and was lodged in Catherine's deep soul. She sat down lumpily on the bed.

Everything mortal dropped away from her. And when thought came clear again it struck her that life was minute and primed with failure, and that she had made very little of it. She had travelled down from the long dreams of her childhood into the fulfilment of trivialities. Everything was trivial and could be closed up in a moment. She saw Cicely watching her. The girl's overstrung voice was hushed at last. She had got it out. She saw in the crushed mute face of the girl a reflection of . . . she did not know what. It made her sorry, sorry for the poor child who had so much yet to lose. 'Cicely,' she said, 'come here!' and when she came she took her into her arms. 'There,' she comforted her, 'you mustn't think hardly of me because I went to the vet. You don't understand. You must try to believe that . . . that everything is on the surface . . . there is only Christy . . .'

'I know! I know! Oh, what are we to do for him!'

'We must never, never, even for a moment, have the least doubt . . .'

Cicely seized her meaning and took it in a different direction: 'We must make it clear. Valentine must go to them and explain . . . after all he is his brother, he has every right to . . . to try to save him in his own way.' As she spoke she stopped crying and looked up at Catherine with wide earnest eyes through wet lashes.

Catherine unfastened her arms. 'Yes. You must find Valentine and tell him. Trust him. Believe that you can trust him, Cicely. Do not let any small-mindedness come between you.'

'I feel,' she confessed, 'that he doesn't like me, nor does Kathleen.'

Catherine suffocated her despair as it came. She thought before she said: 'And even if that is true, Cicely, that he doesn't like you, what has it got to do with it? Likes and dislikes should be far away.'

'I know. I know. You make me ashamed to have thought of them. I feel . . . strong. I will go.'

She had renewed her mission. She would go to Valentine. And in this mood they would surmount dispute and would be friendly. Hope would unite them and effort.

'Go,' she said, 'go now. You may find him. If he comes here I will keep him for you.' It was another part of her madness that their lives should be suddenly without rule; that they should never be able to tell where they could find each other. 'And, Cicely, . . . if you are going to . . . to act as a go-between, try never to let yourself forget that his friends and his own flesh and blood want to save him, not destroy him. Never forget that.' Why should she think of the apostle Peter and hear the cock crowing against a breaking, reddened morning? And then it seemed to her that the apostle Peter had nothing at all to do with it, whether the day came or not, and that with ruthless hands she had stripped this girl before her of youth and innocence. She was standing up before her as a woman with the knowledge of mankind in her changed, resolute eyes. She kissed the young brow. There was no pretence between them. They accepted each other. Leaf by leaf they had turned over into this since a few days ago, since she had seen her standing, distracted and dumb, in the courthouse.

She went with her to the door, kissed her again, and watched her until she turned into the lift at the corner of the green painted wall.

Back in her own room she went, as she had a habit of going whenever she was alone in a room, to the window. It was a front room but too high up to give a glimpse of the street. It looked into a row of shut and blinded windows opposite in a house from which the tenants had departed. It meant nothing to Catherine for she did not see it. She stood before it with her vision inward. She felt intensely feminine, withheld, within, deep in the depths of the soul lay the source of this sweet music. The man who had heard this sweetness was held up above all that was mortal . . . .

She was upheld.

She wanted Christy to be there, instantly there, so that she could take him in her arms as she had taken Cicely, but differently, for she would hold him until the miracle would pass through to him, and he too would hear the voices and be no longer afraid.

Chapter Three

She had the same sensation as of coming out of a theatre at night, into a rainy or very cold night, into a world of bright reflections and people bent upon shelter and destinations, when she went downstairs again amongst people who were either waiting for or on the way to their dinners. Kathleen and André Grenier were sitting on the same seat in the lounge as though they had never moved from it. The electric lights were burning brightly, but unnecessarily, in what was still daylight. The place was familiar to her but grey after the stage from which her spirit came. It was not completely present to her. These two were ghosts who rose to greet her. Christy was no ghost. Her thoughts were his thoughts, measured by the same time and on the same plane, lit by the same colours.

'I thought,' she said, remembering trains, 'that you were going away to-night.'

'I am going to fly across in the morning.'

'He finds flying lyrical.'

There was a song in Kathleen's voice, a song of pain. Her face had a pure, washed look upon it. She had been, perhaps, telling him about Christy. And to know about Christy and find flying lyrical was a form of dimorphism which she found hard to accept. Catherine could accept it without strangeness. And she could understand Kathleen. There was a great tranquillity and steadiness in her whole being as she sat down beside her daughter.

'It must be quite wonderful,' she said calmly, 'to fly through the air . . . like a bird.'

'But you don't, Mother. It's much more like a whale.'

None of them laughed nor spoke.

'In the belly of the whale.' Kathleen laughed herself.

André Grenier turned to Catherine: 'I am so sorry that I should have come under such sad circumstances,' he said in French.

Why should he say it now and not have said it earlier, unless he had said it to Valentine when she wasn't listening? Her eyes acknowledged his intention. The shut tight sweetness turned up the corners of her mouth. 'Where were you when Cicely was here?' she asked Kathleen.

'I haven't seen her. I've been with Dédé all the time, up to now.' She said it defiantly.

'And I,' she said, levelling the defiance, 'have been with Jenny Lysaght . . . all the afternoon.'

Kathleen's hand came down on hers, very cold and tense. 'We went to all sorts of people. Dédé was a great asset . . . his uniform.'

She tried to stop Kathleen with her will. The tone of her voice was much worse to her than Dédé's flying. She remembered Cicely's expression; the change, the sudden finding out of what men could do. And then, quick and sharp, the face of the old woman with the melasmic spot on it: you are his mother. The women on the Calvary mountain. Mary. Mary the mother who hid many things deep in her heart. May God help you! The abandonment of the Father in the Garden of Olives. She stopped these images, this leaping of her mind as a film rolling continuously. Myriorama. Everything was either a dream to her, or this. The peace did not last. A strain in a voice could push the door open and she was out in the open again, lost and wandering. Kathleen withdrew her hand. André Grenier was regarding her as though he had a key to her mind: 'Yes,' she said to him directly, 'I wish that you had come earlier. You will, I hope, come again?'

'Perhaps.'

He would come again, if he came at all, for Kathleen. He would go to Gorabbey. He would be like Mitchell, going there, and she would be absent. Every stone and tree was precious to her there and associated with the life that she had prepared and given to Christy. She could not turn a

corner without a memory of a dark little boy full of wild
burning life, on his pony or flying along on a bicycle,
always doing his lessons at the last moment . . . nominative,
vocative, accusative, genitive, dative, and the flabby, red
cheeked, ponderous tutor clinging to him like a gigantic
mussel, clinging to him for dear educational life. She had
dismissed him because he was so like a blood-sucker.
Christy used to emerge from him untamed, but drained . . .
and afterwards wilder and more daring than ever . . . taking
the boat out in storms and having the sails ripped to pieces
. . . . 'There is a place in Provence that I should like to go to.
It is high up and bare . . . and close to heaven . . . .'

'Mother! I never knew that you had been to Provence!'

'Once, years and years ago, when you were quite little . . .'
before Christy was born, '. . . on the way from Marseilles.'

'Where . . . what place?'

'It is called Lex Baux. There is nothing but rocks.' Then,
as if she had given away a secret, she covered it: 'There are
always many places to which one would like to go.'

'But only one, perhaps, in which one would want to
stay.'

'I haven't found it yet,' Kathleen retorted upon him.

Catherine said: 'Be glad, Kathy, that you haven't,' and
took the sting out of it for André Grenier. It was better
never to find it than to find it and love it and not be able to
remain in it.

Kathleen carried it on: 'I have no sense of place. I'm always
being turned round, blindfold, and going straight on . . . .'

'Perfect,' said Grenier, 'it sounds Euclidean, proving that
the impossible is not impossible.'

'That's it. I'm Euclidean . . . the modern contour.'

Catherine nearly cried out to them to stop, not to play;
and then she was aware that it was not playing. It was a sort
of science, antiseptic, like something that you put straight
on a wound, without bandages. She rebelled against it
although she knew that it was all right. It was drastic, clean,
yet she said: 'Oh! Can't we be . . . real?' And immediately
the sensitiveness showed. André Grenier moved towards a
tiny table, tipped his cigarette ash into a tray that was

placed there, and came back with his face as grey as the ash he had discarded. He said nothing. Catherine was smitten as though in order to save herself she had betrayed them. For one frantic second she was truly in peril, not knowing what she was going to do or say. Kathleen rescued them by standing up, by going back to Euclid: 'The tables in this room are all at right angles . . .' and then, dropping a swift hand on Catherine's shoulder, 'aren't you tired, mother? So tired that you could eat?'

Catherine took the hand and let herself be drawn up. The mere suggestion of tiredness made her conscious of her fatigue. Bodily she felt as heavy and as dull as lead, and oddly irritated by the brooch which she was wearing and could feel through her thin dress. She put her fingers on it and eased it a little but did not undo it. She looked round at André Grenier: 'I think that you two would rather dine alone?'

'But no . . . .'

'But yes . . . and I prefer it like that. I wish to see Valentine . . . .' She looked at Kathleen. She had sent Cicely to him and she knew that they needed her. She was convinced that they needed her. Whatever they were saying to each other, she ought to be there.

They went to the door together. An impulse seized Kathleen, set her alight and kind; 'Dédé! I know a little place in the mountains. They give you eggs . . . in their shells, and pancakes, and there is a candleberry myrtle in a garden perched on rocks over a ravine.'

'Yes,' said Catherine, 'go there! go there!' She matched it against her going with Jenny to see Dickey's bitch and the hopeless darkened dependent woman. But for Kathleen it contained mercy to this young man who loved her. The madness became evident again when she thought that Kathleen called him Dédé and he was still Mr Grenier to her. And she had met him in this hotel. He had not been to Gorabbey. And this was not France where the spirit of acceptance would have mitigated all strangeness. He was so pleased. His bright kindling laugh had run out upon them, full of reward. She hoped that Kathleen would be gentle with him, not clever nor hard. She wanted to say to her: be good to him. When she saw them together she had this instinct to say these sorts of thing to Kathleen, to break down her false feminine defences. They were not needed with him. He gave her a sense of deep tender sincerity as though he lived on the edge of judgements that preserved him from fallacies. Kathleen was far too clever. Beside him she was far too . . . oh, what? Scientific. She cut everything out in the proper shape, her shape.

'Scarpe . . . it is called Scarpe.'

He repeated it, made it significant. She saw olive-dark ivy leaves shining on a wall.

'There are deep blue flowers in the rocks . . . bluebells.'

For Catherine the ivy was translated; she saw the flowers, they sprang clearly out of Kathleen's voice, ringing their mute carillon in the mountain wind; fragile, yet rooted firmly in the bare rock. They had their own world there, up so far above the spears of the spruce-trees. And sometimes the clouds fell below them and lay, powdery and massed, in the valley in lakes of mist. The air was blue like the flowers. One breathed the sky. Dédé . . . Mr Grenier would like it. It would be — lyrical to him . . . .

'Get in, Mother, we will drop you on Valentine's step.'

Hotels and taxis revolved in a wheel of torment, spoke for spoke. She was dislodged. She belonged nowhere except that she returned always to that grill and Christy's hand lost in his dark hair. She put her hand quickly on Kathleen's knee to make sure she was there. Her dress was so thin. 'You have no coat, Kathleen.'

'No. No. I shall not be cold . . . I should like to be cold.' She covered herself with words: 'Haven't you noticed, Dédé, the family habit of using names? We say them on all possible occasions. They replace the dears and darlings which we never use.'

'I like it,' he said with simple directness, 'you can put much into a name.'

'A rose by any other . . .' she pulled herself up, 'you get out here, Mother,' she tapped on the glass. The fool of a man had gone past the door.

Catherine saw the two dark faces welled in the shadow; Kathleen's washed and pure like Monica's against Augustine's. She felt safe for them. Kathleen was not false, only too conscious of the truth. The union was there; they could never really frustrate it. They were bound in it, bound by the love that breaks and mingles. She went up the dusky unlit stairway. Life, when you stripped it to the bone, contained so few meanings, but those few were so great, so profound, that most souls were afraid to face them. Human beings, when they had the chance, did their best to avoid them. But some could not escape. You could be taken out beyond all fear; beyond all courage. You could be taken out beyond life . . . .

She turned the handle of Valentine's door, found that it opened, and went in. In the room beyond, his own room, she found him and Cicely. They had been arguing. They had the exhausted air that comes after tension, the sullen, last lap of resistance. He was sitting on the edge of a table and Cicely on the edge of the deep chair by the fireplace. They both rose, surprise in their voices and eyes. It was just like knocking their two heads together when she said: 'I felt that you two were fighting . . . that is why I came.'

'We were. I've been telling Cicely what I think of her dogmas.'

'Oh, I don't care what he thinks!' Cicely said in desperation.

Catherine looked from one to the other. 'I should think so,' she said wearily, knowing that neither of them would know which one she was answering. The tiredness was on her again, painful. She sat down in the chair that Cicely offered, feeling that she would never be able to rise out of it. 'I don't suppose that it affects Christy.' They were stupid and childlike and she had to be like that with them. Stupid. She preferred Kathleen's shining bright armour. It caught the shafts neatly. This was blundering and bloody. They were both so unhappy. She felt that they were immitigable, beyond reconciliation.

'But it does. It does!'

Valentine's voice seared her through. Oh what could she

say to them? She had come and she could think of nothing to say. Nothing that they could do or say would affect Christy. He was beyond them, beyond good and evil. It was a phrase and she was beyond the phrasemakers. Everything was twisted out in her, wrung, and flung away. She felt white as a sail going through blackness; and though these others could scratch the darkness with lights and symbols she remained white in the blackness, soothed by no sparks of comfort, comfortless. 'If I believe anything, Valentine, it is that only a miracle, a miracle, can save him. A miracle.'

'But Mother! Somebody has got to work it, work the miracle.'

'Yes.' She held fast to the monosyllable.

Valentine, watching her, his will recovering against Cicely and again ready for conquest, saw an expression that resembled light come into her face and possess it. Her face was filled with sweetness, strange and withheld from them, although held there towards them without seeing them. It was sort of transfiguration to him and fascinated him. It had nothing to do with the world from which he and Cicely had disputed in anger. Before it that anger had to be silent.

And from this strange far world Catherine said: 'It's been such a long, long day. The morning is so far away . . . .'

It had been too short for all that he had meant to do with it. He had still to go down to see these people that he and Cicely had been quarrelling about. 'Anyhow, I am going down to see this, this crew, and to see if I can put a stop to their madness, their bestial stupidity. Do you know what they are going to do?'

'No.' She said it to stop him, and with an air of not wanting to hear. Cicely had given her an idea of their intention.

'After having worked up this tremendously signed petition . . . I never . . .' he snapped his fingers, 'gave that for it, they are now going to stop all their support and broadcast that he must be a spy!' His voice sprang a key, 'Because we supported him! Good God, Mother!' He turned to Cicely with the anger renewed and fortified: 'If he gets off we shall not have you to thank.' He did not mean her, personally, but her side, the side she was taking.

The girl stood up to him, mutely, but with all her will.

In Catherine's senses the world turned, showing now Europe, now Asia, Pacific, Atlantic. It was of no consequence what showed. All that mattered was the turning, the passing. All life was modified to her, lessened into its true tiny scope; a bee's life, a man's life — in eternity. And with this measure of eternity she measured Valentine's mood. 'I am going to see Christy in the morning.'

It brought Christy amongst them, gave him the judgment. Valentine's hands became quiet, his body, his eyes; the turbulence was wiped off.

Cicely said: 'Let us try to forget everything except what will be of use.' She meant to him but did not say it.

The opposition lay down in Valentine, deep down. It was like a dog that had been bidden to the corner, obeying for love, the instinct unquelled in him. Valentine felt tamed, chastened by his mother, by this inexplicable quality that illuminated her; but within him the strong male hatred of his enemies burned and glowed and was a torment to him. And he was caught there, as though he had to serve what he hated for the sake of his brother in blood, Christy, who was also the son of his mother. 'Look here, Mother. Will you come with me?' It was the way the influence of her modification worked in him that he should ask her to come and be with him in this meeting with the men he hated with his whole being.

Catherine said nothing. It was terrible to her, like the opening of the doors by the Roman sentries upon the flames of the burning martyrs. The flames scorched her face. She drew back into her silence.

'Oh! do go! Do go with him,' Cicely pleaded, 'otherwise it will be terrible.'

'Terrible!' he mocked at Cicely.

Catherine thought that it was quite terrible as it was. 'But why need it be, Valentine? I trust you.'

'I don't trust myself,' he answered.

The expression on Cicely's face was very like mockery. They both waited for Catherine.

'I would rather not go,' she said simply, 'but if you think that I can be of use by just going, I will come.'

'Yes,' he declared, 'I want you to come.'

Cicely moved a little forward, in front of him. 'And I am coming too,' she announced.

There was another silence. This time the curtain was down and the sentries standing with crossed spears behind it.

'I know that you do not want me, but I am coming.'

She was a new girl to Catherine, knowing what she was doing. Her voice covered her determination with reason, with understanding, with something very like tenderness.

'And I trust you too, Cicely.'

'I know,' she turned from Valentine to Catherine, opening herself, making a gesture of demanding forgiveness: 'Since this afternoon, since you spoke to me (as though Catherine had done it to her) I feel as though I have grown to be an old, old woman.'

'Come here,' Catherine said, and took her hand.

'Yes, I mean it,' she repeated. 'I feel so old, and wise.' From her eyes she bestowed the same plea for forgiveness on Valentine. 'That is why, although you made me angry, I was not truly angry with you . . . but you have, all the same, no right to misjudge me.'

He scoffed at her with his lips and eyes. She pleaded with him and defied him in the one breath. For the flying millionth part of a second he felt savage enough with her to want to wring her neck. And then civilisation came up in him. She was there, by his mother's side. She was greatly to be pitied. 'All right.' He seemed to seal the wisdom upon her, fasten it down with his acceptance. 'And now, if we are going, we had better go at once. What is the address of that rag that you have in your hand?'

She held out the typewritten papers to him. He searched for the address and found it. 'Righto. Well.' He looked at Catherine and, as she did not move, he added: 'We must go.' He gave her his hand and helped to draw her up from the deep chair. The weight she gave against him made him ask: 'You are tired, Mother?'

'Very, Valentine. But I am coming, I am coming.'

'Not if you are too tired,' he insisted.

'I want to come . . . now,' she lied, 'I am quite decided.'

'It is quite near, we must walk, it is only a street or two.'

They walked in silence. The dusk was pooled with arc lamps. The air was heavy as though the twilight had fallen into it from a height, and in this heavy twilight people passed them, in silence and without communication. It was a limbo to Catherine's spirit. She was between two worlds and of neither. Her weariness drugged her senses with pain. The walk to the end of the street was a pilgrimage to her in endurance. And suddenly, at the corner, the limbo went to pieces and a string of motor lorries came rattling past, proclaiming with shrieking horns that it was a world of machinery and an age of noise. She awakened into it with her senses sharpened as the senses of the deaf in a factory.

The newspaper office was on the ground floor of a serious-looking Georgian house. They went into it from a wide hall. Valentine opened the door after a brief rap on the panel and Catherine gently pushed Cicely after him. By going last she would have nothing to say, only to listen. There was a counter, some chairs, and piles of newspapers bound on the floor. A young, piercing-eyed young man asked Valentine his business. She heard Valentine answer brusquely that he was Christy's brother and that he wished to see the chief, Harold Clontarf, immediately.

'You can't do that,' said the young man.

Valentine took him by the shoulder, turned him towards a door marked 'strictly private' and retorted: 'It isn't for you to decide. Go in there and ask him. Tell him that he has got to see me!'

Cicely could not resist looking at Catherine and saying in a low but very audible voice: 'Oh, I hope . . . I hope . . . .'

'Think,' said Valentine, loudly enough to be heard in the next room, 'and don't be a fool.'

An oldish man with abundant grey hair, and wide misty grey eyes under bushy brows was standing on the threshold. He was not tall and his height was diminished by a stoop. He had the face, Catherine thought, of a scholar. He was an idealogue and he had ruled her son. And instantly

he became only an instrument to her. It was not he. It was
the idea. Men were born to the idea as they are born to life.
This man's faith was a race-faith, and ineradicable. 'Come
in please,' he held open the door for them.

They seemed to move all together, to sit all together, to
speak all together as though they were one organism and
not three. The man did not belong to them and the younger
man had returned to the outer office. Catherine knew that
she had not spoken at all, and that the unity was false and
that they were sitting on separate chairs before the
grey-haired tribune. Valentine's voice came out of the
confusion of movement, clear and sharp, with demand:

'I want you to stop this from publication.' He tapped the
papers that Cicely had given him and which he still held in
his hand.

'Where did you get them?'

Cicely said 'from me,' and Valentine said at the same
time: 'never mind where I got them. Are you going to stop
them from being published?'

'I cannot answer that question.'

'You must answer it.'

'I will not answer it.'

Valentine stood up and moved a step threateningly
towards the man who was sitting at the other side of a table.
Catherine felt the rage swell in Valentine as though it was
swelling in herself, bursting her veins. Cicely stood up too.
The man looked under his thatched brows calmly at
Valentine. It was the acquired calm of a man who lived in
an enraged world.

'You have my answer. You had better go.'

The rage slackened in Valentine, controlled. He held his
chin in. 'Do you mean to hang him?'

'It is not we who are hanging him . . . .'

Cicely cried out: 'Oh . . . don't . . . .'

Valentine smothered her: 'Do you mean to say that to
me, his brother?'

'You are his brother in blood . . .' began the tribune, and
stopped, measuring his own denial of brotherhood.

'By God!' exclaimed Valentine, 'I could strangle you, you

deserve it.' But, instantly, he recovered. He took the lead. 'Do you refuse to discuss this with me because you cannot bring yourself to trust me . . . because I am his blood brother?'

'You know that I cannot trust you.'

Valentine's shoulders heaved and went down again. He had the air of dealing with a fractious child, a boy who would not submit to discipline. 'I wish you to disclose nothing. I only wish to convince you that if you publish that article it means certain death to him. If you insist upon the assertion that the government press is pleading for him because he is a government spy do you not realise that you force the government to hang him to prove that he isn't?'

'They are not compelled to hang him, they needn't hang him.'

'You needn't publish that article.'

There was a deadlock. Catherine swung out in it, lost, and retrieved herself. She became articulate: 'Surely,' she said, fixing her gaze on the man who had, so far, shown no feeling, 'in a case like this where a human life is at stake silence would be better than destruction?'

'I live in a world of destruction.'

'You make me aware of it.'

'You are his mother?'

She did not answer him at first, remembering the woman who had asked her in the street. There was no help from man. 'I am his mother. From my body he has been born, born into your world of destruction.'

'I am sorry,' he said.

It was as futile as though he had apologised for God. There was no need to be sorry because she was his mother. The truth was that he was abased before her. The apology was for his own soul.

'I need nothing . . . for myself.' Catherine rebuked him.

'And I . . .' he met her rebuke on some level of his own, 'have nothing to gain by telling you that I can do nothing.'

'You can make an effort,' Valentine bit in.

'A passionate effort,' pleaded Cicely in a voice that was helpless in this cold region.

Catherine remembered, stupidly, Kathleen quoting Dostoevsky. From Siberian prisons . . . the phrase was now rooted in her, part of her life. Her reason was chilled to clarity: 'You can, at least, do nothing?'

'What is nothing to you, may be terrible for us, a crime. It may lead to a greater sacrifice.'

Ah. Then he admitted the sacrifice. 'Come,' she touched Valentine, 'come. It is useless.'

When she said that it was useless, a flame flared in the man, gave him to her. He came round the table, close to her, in front. 'Don't you understand that I am not stone? I, too, have a mother, a wife, sons of my own. But this . . .' he flung out his arms, 'is stronger than mortal love, stronger than mortal life . . . .'

Valentine drew his mother away. 'Are you sure he did it?'

'I don't know. I can't tell you. It isn't a question of individuals, it's a question of, a vital question of policy . . . .'

Valentine's arm shot out and his fist landed close to the man's face. He had not meant to hit him only to threaten him, but Cicely screamed and came between them. She pushed Valentine with all her might. 'You are a fool, Oh! Valentine, what have you done?'

'Nothing!' He shook her off. 'Don't you see I haven't touched him. I wouldn't . . . with my hands . . . .'

Catherine stood still and straight. Her mind was down to bedrock. She felt as Mary must have felt between the Roman soldiers and the apostles. She spoke to Valentine: 'Go. Leave him to me. Go, you and Cicely, go. Wait for me outside. I'll come directly.'

When the door closed behind them the quickness vanished out of her. She turned back to the man as though she did not know what to do with him.

He pulled a chair towards her. 'Won't you sit down?'

His calmness was like doom to her. 'Thank you.' He was grey, broad-shouldered, stooped like Atlas under the burden. She saw banners behind him, flags of all the creeds, crosses of all the faiths. Liberties. Defeats. And he was only a little man, and he spoke her language, spoke it with all its limits. He was defining the limits:

'It is a difficult position.'

'Very,' she answered. How strange to call it that — a difficult position. Like an invalid. She noticed the spiral of the electric light. It was an unusual shape. She turned back to the man, studying him clairvoyantly in all his motives. From a state of prescience she said, as if he had laid bare the map of his 'policy,' 'in your position one would think that . . . that inaction (it was not the word she sought but the word that came) could not be harmful.'

'At our present stage, yes. We must make ourselves felt. We are fighting for our lives.'

He did not, she knew, mean their physical lives, or their bodies, but the life of their cause. She became certain, only in that moment, of the uselessness that she had proclaimed to Valentine. This man was of no use to her. He was of no use to Valentine. She wondered why she had come, why she was talking to him. And it was in justification to herself that she said, proving some purpose before him: 'As a woman all that says nothing to me. I do not believe in destruction. I believe in life before death, spiritual life as well as corporal.

'It is that . . . that spiritual life, if you will, that we are fighting for . . . .' He broke off, looking at her with profoundly felt sympathy.

She could not bear when he argued. 'And my son?' she asked, 'you are' (she was not bitter although the words on her lips were bitter) 'going to sacrifice him for the sake of your policy.'

'We are compelled to,' he lowered his eyes before her.

'It is war.'

'Yes,' he answered her, 'it is war, nothing short of it.'

She stood up again and suddenly remembered that she owed something to Valentine. But what? What? It came. 'And this article. You are going to publish it?'

'It is already with the printers.'

'It is too late.'

She was silent. She sat with her hands limp in her lap. Only one moment, in all the moments to come, could be called too late. Moments. She stood up again, finally,

looking for the last time at the man who was an instrument
in the fate of her son and she had a queer premonition that
one day his own life would be taken. He would fall on a
roadside, the bullets whizzing like pebbles. Grey, and
without shields. Emperors and captains. When a spear fell it
lay dead like the sear of lightning that had passed. Poor
man, she thought towards him, poor man. He knew not
what he did. And those who did, who acted like Valentine
with the weight of days going to a single deed were no less
powerless. In days of war. In days of war. It was with this
phrase ringing through her that she held out her hand,
feeling that in expecting nothing she might, by the same
law of contrariety that operates in children, change his
intentions. 'Then there is nothing to be done.'

He took her hand as though she bestowed a great honour
on him. He had the same pity for her that she had for him.

Pity was the feeblest force on earth. It melted as you used it.

'Even if we use this article it may not have the effect that
you think that it is going to have.'

'No,' she said wearily. It had lasted so long and it had
come to nothing.

When she went outside into the other room she saw
Cicely talking to the nameless young man who had come
out to Gorabbey. She did not see Valentine at first. He was
standing under suddenly blazing electric light close to the
counter beside a man who was counting papers. It
unsteadied her when she saw Cicely and the young man
together and she had another spell of dislodgement, of not
knowing where she was either in time or place. The
dislodgement lasted when, straining her ears and eyes, she
saw and heard him. He was still making the same appeal to
Cicely to persuade Christy to protest in his innocence.
Valentine came to her.

'Well?'

She shook her head. Something went out in his eyes.
'Perhaps,' she comforted him, 'it will not have the effect you
think.' She felt that she had stolen much more than a phrase
from the man in the room that she had left. Cicely was
beside her.

'This man still insists that Christy must take out pleading guilty.'

Valentine wheeled sharply upon the man at Cicely's elbow. 'Did you do it yourself?'

As something had gone out of Valentine's eyes Catherine now saw something come into the young man's eyes. It set her alive again, vigilant. There was a sharp pregnant pause. But when the man's voice came it was cool and steadying. It emptied her again.

'Do you think that if I did it myself I'd be standing here?'

'You haven't said no,' Valentine argued.

'Neither has he.'

She saw Valentine and the young man facing each other in their two moves, everlastingly, in some game that was buried in her heart. She asked, breaking them asunder: 'Where did you come from?' And if he had answered: 'From Gorabbey,' she would have accepted it.

'I was watching you. I saw you come in.'

The night has a thousand eyes. She wished she could stop her mind, stop its intense memory. She was like a drowning man. Every trifle that had ever stamped her consciousness was coming up, floating, passing. She did not belong to any of these men, but she was drowning in their midst. She was going deaf. She saw Cicely gesticulating and she heard nothing coming out of her parted lips. Valentine gripped her suddenly. His grip hurt her. 'Yes,' she assured him, 'yes, I am very tired, I am tired. That is all.' Her hearing came back and she was able to save herself from falling, to stand up-right and walk across the room on Valentine's arm. Cicely followed like a servant, ready and frightened and not daring to touch her. There was nothing to be frightened about. She looked round at her when they reached the dark street and repeated: 'I am tired.'

'I know. Yes, you are very tired.'

The girl's voice was a caress. She didn't mind it. She even did not resent her coming up to her bedroom when they got to the hotel, and helping Valentine to take of her shores. But no further. 'That is all I need. I can get into bed myself. I shall lie down in my dressing-gown. Give it to me,

Valentine, it's hanging up on that nail by the wardrobe, no, not that. The thing with the blue . . . there, that's it.' Kathleen had sent it from Paris, a black silk dressing-gown with blue and red zig-zags.

'Hadn't you better take off your corsets?' Cicely suggested.

'I don't wear them. I never have.' She lay back in the sinking pillows. Valentine covered her feet. Every bone in her body was in pain and the pain was merciful to her nerves. She would let herself give way to it and forget . . .

'What would you like? I don't suppose that you are up to a full dinner. Some soup, or milk? The milk would help you to sleep.'

His hand rested on her feet and she wished that he would take it away. 'I should like some soup. And if Kathleen is there? No. She cannot be back yet. She went to Scarpe.'

'To Scarpe!' They said it together.

'Yes, with André Grenier. Do not think about it, Cicely. You do not understand.' She had to be sharp with her to save her from being stupid. The girl looked suddenly so much older than her twenty years. She need not have been so sharp. But she had been so idiotic over Jenny Lysaght. Oh! You never knew with people. The pain left her no space for analysis. 'Do go and get something to eat, you two. Nothing but soup for me. And tell Kathleen to come up when she gets in, leave a message for her.' She was pushing them out of her room, out of her sight, with these short jerky sentences.

The door had no sooner closed than it opened and Valentine put his head back. 'I'll be downstairs if you want anything. I'll wait until Kathy comes . . . .'

'Are you going out to Gorabbey?'

He hesitated, came in and shut the door. 'Do you want anything brought in from there?'

'No, nothing of any importance . . . I've got enough stockings.' She shut her eyes against what she read in him.

'If I were you, Mother . . . .'

'Now, don't advise me! You know it is useless.

'Yes, but if you could forget . . . .'

'Forget!' She looked at him with full, assessing eyes.

'I know, mother, but if you could . . . those people, just long enough to sleep.'

'I will try.' She was moved, but from a long distance, by him. Not close. He was kind, but individual, separate. The family feeling was there, deep and rooted, there was no need to gather words from it. Words were a cloak; they were like the keys of music boxes which turned and set a tune going. It was not always the tune you wanted, or you knew it by heart.

And as soon as he went and she had made certain that he was not immediately coming back to her she let herself go, gave herself up to the pain. If only she could die, be certain that this pain would end in death, she would be full of courage. Death would release her. If only she could lie between the sheets knowing that her hours, like Christy's hours, were numbered, what magnanimity would enter her then. This morning she had felt ready to bear the whole burden; yesterday too. Centripetal. Drawing them all into her own upright strength. And now she was scattered, centrifugal, and they were each separate and concentrated in their own shells and she was of no use. She had failed with the man. She had failed.

There was neither flight nor future.

She would live by going backwards. The return journey, picking up the traces and putting them, like flowers into a basket, into the receptacle that her life had been. Mitchell and the hawk. The age of falconry rammed into a page of Washington Irving. Every drop of Druid blood in their beings warmed and quickened again when they piled the stones on the mountain. Nobody had ever taken Mitchell's place and he himself had never refilled it. Her father had tried through long winter evenings and from the pages of books; looking at her with the eyes that had since become her own and saying (in the low family voice): 'there have been three miraculous births — Gautama, Mahomet and Christ. Three leaves on the stem. One birth in the roses and the other in the manger. By such strange portes do Gods come upon earth.' Going into it as into a room full of people all waiting and ready to believe in them. They were born from the belief. You could enter heaven by the sword, or by love. The love was nothing in itself. She saw a white rose-bush with blood-veined leaves.

Once, when he was a small boy, Christy had caught a corncrake and shut it into the drawing-room. It ran round and round keeping close to the four walls, craking for the fields of ripening grain from which it had been taken.

He had those strong brown hands even then with the index finger closed in a circle against the thumb like a priest after he has touched the Eucharist. He pointed at everything with the middle finger, the political finger.

She was going to see him in the morning. She had a queer, biting feeling that she had not seen him since he was a little boy. So much could pass away in a few days. Only a few days.

The hotel maid came in with her soup. She sat with the tray on her knees, dipping the spoon into the celery soup and learning the hotel monogram: blue, interlinked esses. She was too tired to eat her soup but she ate it. She began to go over Christy's clothes; his grey suit, his blue, the homespun, his plus fours and pull-overs, his flannels. He never wore blue shirts like Valentine, and his ties were always tied far too tightly. She saw his hands tugging them. And he could never shave himself without a scratch. He did everything too quickly. No patience.

They had caught him at a meeting. He had listened. He had walked down the rainy road with Cicely. Saul from Tarsus had walked down a road. She, herself, had walked down the mountain the day that Mitchell had gone. And she had married Luke. She had refused him five times and the sixth accepted him. The first time that he had taken her into his arms and held her close she had felt that it was a betrayal of Mitchell, who was already married. She had given herself to Luke with the same feeling. It had been stronger than the truth. Valentine and Kathleen had been born from this reserve, the fire all on Luke's side. It was only with Christy that she had begun to live as a woman, to know motherhood. She had felt royal when she was carrying Christy, proud in the possession of her kingdom, creative, holding all life within her womb; dark as plants under the load of winter. The earth, by then, had truly got her, and she went with its plan, functioning in harmony with every living creative organism. She had loved her husband. She had been happy and the child she was bearing had been contained in this intensity. She had gone deep down to the root of life, to the core of all growth. He had lain to one side and when she had put her hand there she had felt him . . . .

She could feel him all over again as she lay there on the bed. It did not seem to be all those years ago. He was a young man. You do not know, she thought to him, how much of your life has been my life. He had come in her highest tide, a flood. The breaking of the waters. Beautiful as poetry in the old testament. No false shames, no virginal horrors, but a ripe woman knowing the reason and purpose of life and standing up to her share in it.

In thinking of him she had this great desire to draw him back again into the shelter of her own being. His body was beyond her power but his spirit! That was within the scope of her cry. Last night she had possessed him. He had sent her a message that was a sign.

Yes. She would preserve him. She would surround him with wings that would shut out terror. Her flight would be his, his hers.

His clothes would hang, emptied forever, in the cupboard in the room from which he was already absent. Cicely had gone in there yesterday like a little tiny insect, not knowing where to alight, finding no pollen.

Luke had never known about Mitchell. But once, when they had met Mitchell accidentally in that place in the Spanish Pyrenees, turning the corner of a dusty scratchy road above a valley flaming with yellows, he had had a vague comprehension, a wind passing through his soul as though something had had to be acknowledged. They had all gone to see Jenny Lysaght who was there for her lungs. Mitchell had covered it up: 'Well, this is a great treat! Paddy is coming up for the day, from his school in Pau.' He was all in white as though he had stepped across from China. And he had pulled out a silk handkerchief and squashed it up and let it bounce out of his hand showing the fangs of dragons, yellow against blue. She had said: Show it to me, and he had given it to her to look at the design and stop her heart from battling with her sense and find something to say that would clear her eyes enough to look straight at Luke who was watching. She knew that he was watching although she kept her eyes on the dragons in the handkerchief. She had said, in the end, and not too casually, 'Valentine is going to be as tall as Paddy?' She never thought of Valentine's height without remembering it as text against the picture of the silk dragons and Mitchell's voice, and Paddy coming up so alliteratively from Pau.

Somebody was knocking and she felt too far away to want to answer. She lay silent and they knocked again and Cicely came in, on tip-toe as though certain that she slept. 'I am awake,' she said.

'Is there anything that I can do, that you would like?' She stood half-way between the door and the bed.

'Nothing. Nothing. You must go to bed . . .'

'I am going home.'

'But it is late. It must be after ten o'clock.'

'It is nearly eleven, but my uncle insists. My aunt does not wish to stay in the hotel . . . .'

With us, Catherine finished her sentence. The girl looked very tired. The young air had wilted in her. She felt sorry for her but cold about it, cold as she had felt about Valentine when he had been so gentle with her. It did not matter. It could wait. It was one of the many things that could wait. 'Kathleen hasn't come in?'

'No. Valentine is waiting for her.'

'He needn't wait. If he leaves a message . . . tell him to come up.' She thought quickly: shall I want anything from Gorabbey or not? Which would be easier for him? Nothing. I shall say nothing. 'Good-bye, Cicely, until the morning. Try to sleep. You are going to see him in the morning?'

'I don't know. I hope so. So many people may want to see him in the morning.'

'Yes. I suppose so.' She would not wait for Redmond. She would go early before any of them. She gave her cheek to Cicely who suddenly stooped over her. And she again had that terrible feeling of dislodgement, of being swung out in space. Nothing was familiar. Nothing had any associations. This girl had no right to kiss her. The room was strange, even her clothes which were on the chair, hung up on the nail, were not like her own clothes but like the clothes of some voyager who was passing through her life. 'Go,' she said as the girl still stood, indecisive.

She waited for Valentine, who rapped and entered at the same time.

'Good-night, Valentine, don't wait. Tell them to tell Kathleen to come into my room whenever she comes in. I shall not be asleep.'

'But you ought to, to try to.'

She let it pass. She regulated the fringe of the coverlet which was pulled over her knees. Valentine was taller than Paddy and Paddy was dead. He was the one who had acted most, who had performed the greatest efforts. 'When do you think that Redmond ought to hear from the Home Secretary?'

He leaned his knee against the bed, jerking her a little and moving all her joints. His eyes paled, or pallor went through them. But his voice came steadily and without hesitation, almost as if he had thought out the answer to this question. 'To-morrow, I expect. That is why I wanted to hold those brutes back.'

'I don't suppose that they are brutes . . . more than the rest of us.'

'No. By heaven they are very human. It depends upon the degree of humanity.'

He was sarcastic, and quite ready to bite her. That seemed strange to her too, and very foreign. He looked suddenly handsome and distinguished and like a man whom she was only getting to know. 'Then . . . to-morrow.'

The pallor in his eyes now was full of pain, hiding something distorted: 'To-morrow . . . of course we may not . . . .'

She broke in purposely, preventing him: 'Don't wait, Valentine. It is already late.'

He was relieved and not wanting to show it. He put his arm across her body, and, leaning on the bed on his two hands, he bent his face close and kissed her. He kissed her as though he cared for her, cared what happened to her: and for one tiny second the coldness shook as though touched by heat and became solid again, stolid — beyond response. 'I'll tell them downstairs about Kathleen. And this Grenier fellow . . . you like him?'

'Yes, I like him. I don't know anything about him, but . . .' she searched, 'he is quite one of us, wouldn't you say?'

'Quite.' He looked at his reflection in the mirror, pushed his collar down with a forefinger, and turned back to her. 'I'd like a bath but it's too late . . . .'

'Not for the hotel.'

'No. I shan't bother. I'll go now. I hope you'll get some sleep. At any rate you're resting.'

'Yes, I'm resting.'

It was over and she was alone again. She was stretched out, that was certain . . . resting. He wouldn't take a bath. He did not mind going to the girl without a bath. He was dreadfully upset, keeping it in for her sake. He wasn't so egoistic after all, Valentine. He could think of others. But with the girl she imagined that he hid nothing, kept nothing in. She was so evidently that sort, if he could go to her without a bath. She would comfort him, release the anguish in him. But this question of contraception. She had never been able to accept it and never would. There was something vulgar about it, like consciousness where no consciousness ought to be. And what else was there for them to do? The tribal days were over. Children were legal individuals from the moment of their birth and no longer part of the tribal packings. Strays, yes, on the street . . . fed out of the rates! Something always wrong with their eyes. Yes, that had to be ended. It was, of course, quite wise to decide about children — whether you were to have them or not. It was incredible to her that, with his special character, Valentine should ever be caught in that decision. He despised traps. He would, she had always thought — until this happened, take parentage and marriage if anything too seriously. But those sorts of men could often play with a girl, wade through legions of them into powerlessness over some woman that would make them want to marry her. He would never have wanted to marry Cicely . . . .

She felt sleep coming and accepted it, hoping that it would last until Kathleen came in. She turned off the hard bulb of light.

She dreamt of going down a long endless corridor in an endless quest. She woke into greyness to hear Kathleen's voice. She felt weighty as lead in the bed: 'Come in. Turn on the light.' It came suddenly and blinded her. She blinked into understanding of Kathleen's stare.

'Mother! didn't you undress?'

Well! What of it. She had just dozed off. 'That's nothing. I'm going to undress now.'

Kathleen still stared. 'I've just got up . . . to have breakfast with Dédé. He's going in half an hour.'

She had slept and the night had been a moment. And she had never moved. She had waked in the same position. 'What time is it?'

'About half past six. I didn't come in last night, or rather this morning, Mother. I didn't want to disturb you.'

'It wouldn't have disturbed me. But I expect it was just as well that I slept. But I should have liked you to come in, Kathleen.' Some instinct made her say it and immediately her mere saying it became a key in Kathleen's face. 'What has happened . . . between you and Dédé?' She ought not to have asked. It came out, and she was not quite awake or she would have been able to control it.

'Nothing. Absolutely nothing.'

Kathleen did not understand. She was answering another question, one that she had not asked. She let it go. She was awake now and she was going to see Christy. She forgot Kathleen. It was only when she spoke again that she remembered that she was still there.

'I am going. I am going to share his last breakfast.'

His last! But he had arrived yesterday after breakfast. Kathleen's face was a mask again, beyond the edge of her scrutiny, perfect in its control. There was nothing to be told.

She looked calmer, that was all. He had come and he was going, and partings were always terrible . . . .

'Say good-bye to him for me. I like him so much, Kathleen, I hope that we shall meet again.'

'Perhaps you will. He likes you too.'

She lay there without moving after Kathleen had gone. She knew that she would have to get up and undress a little and wash and dress again and have some breakfast too. She was going out. The foxgloves on the wall-paper were very full. She searched vainly for a word ending with ent which would express the fullness of the foxgloves and did not find it. Digitalis. You put them on your fingers like thimbles . . . fairies' thimbles. They were all wrong on a white ground and anyhow far too bright for a bedroom paper. They belonged to the hedges, in a hedge's shadow, amongst the green-pointed roofs of the leaves. They were living, the flowers; they sprang from seed and rose and blossomed and died. She tried to think of something that was not living, and beautiful . . . the grains of stones. Turquoises when they had begun to perish, with the grey lights turning the blue to green. The tiles at Les Baux and that arch in Bernard's yard with the ditriglyph parted like a spray of stone, granulated, weathered into tiny cups that held the rains.

She wanted to think of nothing else but Christy, and her mind would wander, like the soul from prayer, away from him.

She rang, ordered her breakfast when the maid came and told her that she wanted the telephone number of Edward Redmond's private address. She had breakfast in her room and went down ready dressed to go out. She rang up Redmond and was told that he was in his bath. She had to wait, like Charlotte Corday, until he could speak to her. Kathleen, they told her, had gone out with the gentleman. She sat with an impatience that grew until she could stand it no longer. She decided not to wait but to go direct to the gaol. After all, I am his mother, she thought, they cannot refuse to let me see him.

There was nobody in the street. In the laurels at the edge of the small park in front of the hotel a wren was singing its tiny trilling hymn of gladness, of life. It had brought up its young. It was blessed by the quiet morning. A thin mist of coming heat lay over the bushes. By the railings on the Eastern side of the park a cripple was selling newspapers. He was tying the early posters on to the railings. Catherine turned sharply away from him down a street on her right where people in a thin stream were pouring out from early mass in Saint Anastasia's. They had an air of having dressed in their sleep; but their eyes, when she met them, had something shy and bright and uncurious in them. They were believers. They were coming from the shrine with the belief strong in their souls, in their hearts, in their shy furtive eyes — the eyes of people who have truly something to hide. Give me a share in your prayers, she prayed as they passed her; I am a woman in need. And for the first time in her life she understood their secrecy. She had been in that realm from which such secrecies spring.

When she came to the church she went in. She passed through dark leather doors into the dark sheltering church and knelt down. The sanctuary lamp was burning in two shades of red — from the flame within it and the daylight without. It shone like a precious stone in the space above the tabernacle doors. An old man crept out of a seat in front of Catherine, and made a long genuflection before the Divine Presence. The prayers in Catherine's soul would not rise to her lips. She was conscious of the large crucifix and kept her eyes away from it. In avoiding it her gaze went full into a painting of Mary before the embalmed body of her son. She was transfixed and stirred, devastated by understanding. It was so much older than she, this happening, this — leaving of the mother. They took him down from the cross and Mary hid many things in her heart. How many mothers had hidden things in their hearts! Men died and women stayed on after them to learn the full meaning, the bitter, unsatisfying taste of life . . . the life they had created.

Civilisation had accomplished several ways of escaping the lesson. Women could escape motherhood, and Medea-like get things all their own way. But only for a time, only for a time. Even if the end clashed down with cymbals, with trumpets blowing, it was still the end. It came.

Before the stricken figure of Mary she was humiliated as a woman of her age; and her grief lessened, and distanced within the scope of the whole world's record of her experiences. She was not the only one. It was continual and there were always others. Her heart broke then against life, broke completely. She bowed her head down on her hands, resting there without movement. She was an instrument and she had been used; and if there was a resurrection and a life to come then her soul could go out to it scraped clean and burned out into eternal fitness. She did not know, but whatever unity was meant by God she was desolated into its need.

All that spiritual life which people kept secret became a kingdom of refuge: a sea in which was washed away all terrors.

The scoffers and the indifferent seemed very little and remote to her and their courage was like the courage of flies. The pattern of Life was too great for their indifference to matter more than a leaf in a corner, more than the salute of an army. It didn't matter how you held up your hands.

There were masses of marguerites on the virgin's altar. Not for the statue. She understood now. It was not the statue, not the image but the long-preserved idea, the fertile trap of life. It was done through love. The bitter discipline came through love. Manhood and womanhood went in two directions until love made the woman follow . . . .

Her thoughts seemed in that brief interval in the strange church, to lose their raggedness. She was no longer torn to ribbons in a storm, she was anchored.

She went to the gaol in this quietness of spirit. The warder would not allow her to see her son without a permit. She asked to see the governor and was shown into his dining-room where he was having breakfast. He stood up for a moment when she came in, begged her to be seated and continued to serve himself with ham and eggs.

'You are his mother?'

'Yes.' She wondered how many times she was going to

be asked that. It made her feel heavy and sit on the chair as though she had no animation, as though she had been thrown there. Would he or would he not? She could not ask him again.

He looked at her as though he expected to be asked again, and when she said nothing, he put the yolk of an egg into his mouth. His voice was sharp when he spoke: 'It is unusual . . . he has had many visitors, with permits, I mean . . . but as you are his mother. How many times have you seen him since he was condemned?'

'Once.'

He sent her a swift shrewd glance. 'You disapprove . . . you do not approve of his ideas?'

She sat there, staring at him, wondering what to say. What did it matter what she thought! He was grey, ponderous, a little like the man in the newspaper-office to her. He functioned in a world where her spirit could not enter. She answered, like a catechism: 'He is my son.'

He took a piece of toast out of a silver rack, buttered it, bit a piece out of it, munched, and with the masticated morsel still in his mouth said, 'Well, I suppose so. I suppose you are all right. I can trust you? You will not see him alone.'

'I know.' There was, even now, a warder outside the door.

He fumbled in his pockets, brought out a pad, his fountain pen, and wrote her a permit.

She went down the carpeted stairs after the warder, across the prison yard to the corridor and staircase of stone that was already known to her. The clean summer sunlight lay in rays across the stone passages. All this, these walls, these stones, had been built by human hands. She was reminded of the stone of the Bastille in Paris which had been preserved and was now a Montsouris. Mice ran where thoughts had run in despair. Prisons were still there. The King is dead, long live the king. She kept her eyes down, on the warder's shiny heels and his narrow blue trousers-ends. She did not want to see Christy until he saw her nor surprise him — too much. It was when she came right up to his cell that she raised her eyes and looked. It was she who suffered the surprise. She was caught, but differently, as she had been caught by the picture of Mary. They had shaved him. They had shaved off his dark hair.

It pierced her with revelation, stabbed her as though she had come upon them weaving his shroud. Her throat was parched so that when he cried her name she would say nothing, only look at him as though, like Mary's son he lay on her knees . . . .

'I wasn't expecting you so early . . . Mother!'

She got her voice out: 'I came, I had to come before all the others.'

'Mother . . . don't mind . . . .'

His eyes looked enormous and full of vision, reading her. She put her fingers against the grill, touching him: touching him with her consciousness beyond her finger-tips. 'Don't,' she pleaded quietly, 'tell me not to mind.' There was such a little time left. They must not waste it.

'For you . . . I would give anything . . . .'

She looked away from him. She could not help him. She thought distractedly, losing her wits for a moment. The moment went over her when, making an effort out of it, she returned to that desolated interval of the church when she had been humbled out of her sorrow. It helped her to cover the harsh dryness in her voice: 'I did not expect to see you with your hair cut.'

'No,' he laughed a little dry laugh, 'they did it yesterday, late in the afternoon.'

'Late in the afternoon.' Where was she yesterday afternoon? What had she done? Gone to Redmond's with Cicely, after Jenny had left her. 'Yes . . . what does that mean?'

'I suppose . . .' this time there was no laugh, 'it may mean . . . anything . . . or nothing.' She was looking so intensely into his eyes that when the expression broke in them it broke in her own too. It broke her completely out of every thought of herself, of her own feelings. She felt only for him. She had an insufferable desire to reach through the barrier and take him into her arms, to comfort him, to give him strength. 'My thoughts have been full of you,' was the nearest she got.

'I have felt them.'

It was as though he had buckled armour on her. She rose, ready to carry him on her spirit, to make that spirit strong enough to bear him.

'The why and the wherefore do not matter . . . now.'

'I know that, Mother. I feel that with you, only with you.'

His nails had black edges. His skin looked tired, full of the strain he had been suffering. These little bodily trifles, of no consequence. She possessed him beyond them. 'On my way here I went into a church . . . a catholic church.' He was silent, drawn closer than any physical touch. 'I did not pray. I could not, but I had a strange calmness there, Christy.' It was difficult for him to follow her. He had not been there. He was lost on the heads of her words; but deep down there was a response in him. And he had felt her thoughts. 'It was queer, Christy . . . ' and suddenly he surprised her with comprehension.

'Like looking at things far up, far away.'

'Exactly.'

They exchanged their understanding, mutely, in a brief startling pause.

He revealed himself: 'I used to talk about that, about religion to Cicely.'

A few weeks ago she would have had a sense of robbery. She would have been down on Cicely, suspicious. She did not think of anything base now, she was accepting essentials. She gave him revelation for revelation. 'I think that, perhaps, we have been too reserved about religion. I was a child, Christy, at a time when the scientific mind was beginning to rise for a great flight. Anything that could be regarded as superstitious was scoffed at. Saints were on the same plane as wizards.'

'You believe in saints?'

'Yes, I do.'

There was another brief pause, out of which he said simply: 'I believe in God.'

She was as contented as if he had made a meeting-place for them in certainty, in heaven. But all she said was: 'It will be a comfort to you.'

'Anyhow the saints had the courage to face death . . .'

He was thinking of the martyrs. She said in a voice deep with love, smiling at him, 'you aren't a saint, Christy.'

'Oh, Mother, I know!' His laugh had a true ring in it.

They were united, understanding each other. She felt full towards him, her arms full of flowers, of thoughts, of known things, of all that she had given him in life. 'Before you were born, Christy, I was happier than I had been with all the others.'

'Mother!'

'You have always been very close to me.'

He made a restricted, inarticulate sound; controlled it into words. 'I haven't given you much.'

She stopped him. 'You have been. That has been sufficient . . . for me. I should like, Christy, for it to be sufficient for you.' She knew that it was a trap for him.

'That's just it, Mother. I can't get myself into resignation. I . . .' he knew that he could give her the bare truth. 'I don't want to die.'

Die at the right moment. She searched her wits for what to say. 'Don't be afraid . . . .'

'I'm not afraid. I just do not want to die, to go out like that.' He snapped his fingers in the same way as Valentine.

'In the church this morning,' she said slowly, measuring her own meaning, 'I felt that we were not alone, that this, all this we are feeling now, has been felt, and suffered over and over. We belong . . . spiritually to a communion . . . the communion of saints, can you understand, Christy?'

He thought it out. 'I would call it God.'

'Yes.' It was simpler. It ended there.

'It isn't, Mother, that I want to pray, to say prayers that one has learned, but to offer myself, thoughts . . . .'

'And isn't that prayer?'

'I suppose it is.'

The warder made a sign to her that the time was up, or that he had had enough. Perhaps they changed guards, or he wanted his breakfast or something. It could not be important, so she took no notice. She pretended that she had not seen. 'I am glad that we have talked like this. When your grandfather died, Christy, he died suddenly, in the night. The funeral was very simple. He did not believe in ritual of any sort. And it was quite difficult because he had left instructions to be buried face downwards. He said that he would like to feel that, that he could use his hands. I had the greatest difficulty in having my, or rather his, way about it. Then when your own father died I wasn't there. He was, as you know, on a visit to Mitchell. But now . . . and I have sometimes thought of my own death, I have begun to feel that it is terrible to go out like that . . . .' Like her father on his face. 'Mitchell has always said that death to us here is birth to us elsewhere and that we have no right to enter another state as though we were flung there.'

It was stopped for her. The warder put his hand across her, touching her repulsively. And although he had been there all the time and had heard everything the mere fact of his touch prevented her from further speech. It was driven under again into mute rays of feeling.

Christy said, after a minute in which they belonged silently to each other: 'You'd better go, Mother, good-bye . . . you know it means God be with you.' His smile had a wonderful light in it, catching her heart in its flight.

'And with you, too.'

The calmness stayed on her, strange, mystical. They had spoken of unpremeditated deep-lying things. Although she went from him she felt no break. She was aware that he felt none too, that they stayed near to each other in absence and communication. She felt strong, washed. Washed in the blood of the Lamb. This was what they meant and it was beyond ridicule. Every simple peasant-thought was acceptable. And when they said, giving you a flower: take it, it means good-luck, it only meant that some human soul had worn it in triumph.

When she went into the street again it was like returning to a plain country from which she had long been absent.

In the hotel she found Kathleen waiting for her. She came to greet her immediately she entered the vestibule. 'Where have you been, Mother?'

'I've been to see Christy.'

'Mother . . . no! Not so early?'

She assured the fear behind Kathleen's eyes. She was quite sane. She did know what she was talking about. 'Yes, it was very early. I had a little difficulty, but I was fortunate enough to catch the governor before he began his round for the day,' (she saw him wolfing his ham and eggs) 'and I was allowed to see him.'

Kathleen said: 'Let us sit down. Have you had breakfast?'

'Yes.' They found a quiet seat, hidden by palms. The room was empty and the waiters were going about with a fresh expectant air.

'How is he . . . still in good spirits?'

She could not tell Kathleen that they had shaved him. 'He was calm.'

Kathleen stretched out towards a table and turned over a magazine that lay there. Then suddenly she got up and went over and stood by the window looking out on to the street. Her back was tragic to Catherine, helpless. She had always liked her in that particular coat and skirt. She came back. 'Mother. I think I must look at a paper.'

The look they exchanged was significant. 'Ask a waiter.'

'No, I prefer to go out and buy one.'

Their eyes again revealed the reason. She watched the graceful quiet poise of Kathleen's form go down the room and round the screen. She sat there with her hands in her lap. She began to think with a quick startling wildness of what might be in the paper, and with such force that it was insupportable. Before she really knew what she was doing she was hurrying down the room after Kathleen, calling her by name.

'I'm coming with you!'

Kathleen waited, her brows furrowed. They went out together. Catherine remembered that she had taken the pins out of her hat. She had been thinking of taking off her hat when she had the abrupt idea to run after Kathleen. She had stuck the pins into the upholstered chair. 'I . . . don't walk so fast, Kathy, my hat isn't pinned on.'

'Don't try to keep up with me, walk slowly, I'll run on and get a paper. There's a man here at the corner.'

It was the same man who had been tying up his posters a little earlier. Instead of walking she stood, watching Kathleen, fascinated with suspense. She saw her buy the paper, open it and scan it quickly. She knew that she would not blunder or miss what she was looking for. Kathleen came back, and when she was half-way towards her she looked up and saw her and waved the folded paper, a tiny re-assuring wave that told her that there was no disaster. Her throat hurt her then, and looking away quickly as though it was necessary to hide from Kathleen that her throat was hurting her she saw a boy wheeling another boy in a hand-cart. The hand-cart and her emotions were matched in her consciousness into an image of a tombereau going to the guillotine, and she was linked to the Terror and swung back by another proof that she was no solitary; that others all through the earth, had gone along the same road of agony.

'There is . . . nothing.'

She meant nothing definite. They went back to the hotel. Kathleen left the folded paper, through which she had so barely glanced, on a table as she passed. They went to the same seats and Catherine took off her hat.

Kathleen said: 'Valentine told me last night . . . about the revolutionary development.' (She meant the affair with Harold Clontarf.) 'So that is what they are worth!'

'I shouldn't call it worth,' Catherine rebuked, 'nor measure them by their mistakes.' She was in no mood for judgement.

'You are very generous, Mother.'

It wasn't generosity. It wasn't pity nor forgiveness nor charity. She tried to comfort Kathleen: 'It may not mean anything.'

'He gives his life and they deny him! It could only happen in this country.'

'It always happens,' she said quietly against the girl's bitterness.

'Yes, but they've overdone it here . . . .'

She dreaded cleverness, and the analytical manner in which Kathleen's mind worked when she got on to this

subject. In order to avoid it she asked: 'Did Valentine tell
you last night if he was coming here first thing, perhaps he
will go direct to Redmond's, if so we ought to go there.'

'No, and just before you came in I rang him up at
Gorabbey. I was anxious about you. He wasn't there.'

She knew. It did not surprise her. She was aware of the
pause and the question in Kathleen's eyes, and filled it: 'He
may have left early, got up early . . . like us.'

Kathleen's lips smiled slowly from her lips, twisted a
little, 'Oh, no, he didn't. He hadn't been there all the night.'

She said nothing. They sat there in an honesty towards
each other that would not play. And, looking up, she saw
Valentine coming towards them, 'Why! There he is! And
Kathy, if I were you, I wouldn't, just now . . .' He was there.
He kissed her.

'Well!' his voice was breezy, too breezy, 'the papers are
all right. Nothing yet.'

Catherine knew too well that it was too early to expect
the reaction to the article, if the article had been published.
She dreaded knowing, yet she found herself asking: 'Did
they' (she meant the grey misty-eyed man) 'publish it?'

'Yes. Last night, late. Their news often flies about
midnight. This had got pretty well ahead.'

So he had published it. It amazed her to discover that she
had been trusting him not to, and that she had faith which
could again be broken. She said by rote: 'It may make no
difference.'

Neither Kathleen nor Valentine answered her, and she
realised that she was repeating these comforting denials,
like an actor in rehearsal, to keep the others going. A few
days ago she would not have been able. It occurred to her
that they were like a drove of sheep on the threshold of the
shambles; the green familiar fields, the familiar skies so far
away. The cries and the panic were exhausted and fear at its
flood in them. They could sit still now. They could say these
things.

'I'll go and have a snack of breakfast, hadn't time . . .' he
patted his bulging pockets, 'all these papers to look
through. Will you wait here for me?'

They would wait. They sat in silence until the silence had to be broken. Kathleen said: 'So André Grenier has gone.'

She had not called him Dédé. 'I liked him so much, Kathleen. I should like to meet him again.'

'Perhaps you will, Mother.'

Another silence in which the Yucca leaves came out in the corner of the carpet under the brown leathered feet of a man who passed. It was again Kathleen who spoke.

'It was lovely last night, at Scarpe, unforgettable.'

Catherine turned, aware, beyond the beauty of Scarpe, of heartbreak in Kathleen's spirit. It was clear to her as though she had been told. The girl's profile told her nothing. 'It was the right place to take him.'

'Yes.'

'He will, perhaps, come back . . .' It was again rehearsal. Better to say nothing. But this time it worked. The trouble, whatever it was, seethed in Kathleen, melted her. She broke, and turned with such passion controlled in her low voice that Catherine's hand sprang towards her:

'He will never come back! Never!'

'Kathy!' She had known it all along. It made the girl little again, dependent upon her. Yet she could not touch her. It was years since she had held Kathleen in her arms. Here, in this strange hotel the reserve had to be kept up, anybody might pass . . . .

All she could say was: 'It was such a dreadful time for him to come.'

'Oh, Mother, I don't know. I don't understand. I love him differently from Christy, I want him, in my life, as I never could want Christy, and yet this . . . this about Christy has killed everything else. Nothing else matters. Do you know,' she looked at Catherine with eyes in which pain and reason were strangely mixed, 'I have sent Dédé back to his wife and for two years I've been begging him to leave her!'

'Oh!' she was blind again, down in darkness.

'It was here, only now, that he offered to divorce her. He found me so unhappy. He came . . .'

'He came,' she repeated, and measured the man's love.

'Yes. He was splendid. He is like that.'

And he was religious, deep. Catherine trusted him. 'What was it . . . with his wife?

'It was an arranged marriage, made to keep some lands together.' She thrust her arms forward, linked her fingers together and drew them in a vice against each other: 'Oh, what is it, Mother? I don't understand . . . it is the end of everything, nothing matters, or can matter again . . . only Christy . . . .'

And Catherine, understanding, knowing too deep for speech, sat there in silence.

'He has gone away. I have sent him away.'

Catherine began no comfort with 'perhaps.' Here was another thing to hide in her heart, to make room for, and bear . . . for these children whom she had begotten.

Chapter Four

Above the olive green carpet, through the olive green furniture, between the olive green walls Valentine came back from his snack of breakfast to where Catherine still sat with Kathleen. The hotel was marked down in her in that short space of time as the waiting-room for her last voyage, the return journey. The shell of her individual meaning broke there and her soul was shattered. Only for a very little while would she have the power to use herself. Afterwards she would be used, as one uses inanimate things, by others.

Valentine said: 'I would rather go to Redmond without you.'

'Well, do go,' she answered.

But Kathleen resented him: 'No, I'm coming with you. I must, I must see Christy to-day. It is his last day . . . .' She broke off, regretting instantly what she had said in her passion — what none of them had been able to say, and her eyes ran from her mother, finding out how she had taken it, to Valentine. 'Oh, Valentine, I must see him.'

'But of course you will see him.' His voice not only assured her on that score but carried in it a promise of further fulfilment. His hope was unshaken by any personal disaster. 'And you, Mother?'

'I have already seen him . . . this morning.'

The amazement ran through him and became ominous. 'Mother!'

She covered his meaning, sheltered him. 'It is all right, Valentine. I was up so early. I have not, you know, seen much of him.' Cicely had seen him every time.

'How was he . . . cheerful?'

'He was calm.' The same hiding answer. Kathleen went

on sitting. Valentine still stood. She released them. 'If you like I will not come. I do not need to come, nor want to.' Redmond had promised to let her know immediately when he heard. She trusted him. At once, as she spoke, she knew that she could not bear to wait in the hotel. But where was she to wait? Where was she to find them all again? She could not stay alone. They would be going to the gaol! 'I think, I think that I shall go down to the gaol again . . .' she comforted Valentine, left him free for his plans, 'to wait for you. You,' she turned to Kathleen, 'will be going there. I should like to wait for you there . . . to be near him . . . even if I don't see him. I do not suppose that they will let me see him again . . . just yet.'

The relief that came into their attitudes was almost like a conspiracy. She ignored it. She sat on after they had gone, for several minutes, until she was certain that they would not see her, then she got up and went out.

She paused as she passed the church and wondered if she should go in again. The revelation there could not be repeated, or rather she was afraid that it would not repeat itself, and anything else would break its peace for her. She stood on the pavement breathing thanks for it, for the grace it had brought her: and continued, caught again by its mercy.

The warder let her enter. She told him that she was obliged to wait for somebody who was coming there. It did not matter what she said so long as she convinced him of her need to be there. Perhaps he did not need much convincing. He knew her by now. She knew his brusqueness, his professional air of terror which meant nothing at all to her.

She sat on the same stone bench at the foot of the stairs where she had waited for Kathleen and Cicely. The bare stony place had a fitness for her. It was not incongruous like the hotel; it did not mock her. It bound Christy in with a stern strength, and it bound his meaning in the same fashion. There was no way out of it. She sat, quiet, knitting the threads of what Kathleen had told her. He was going out there, to danger, this André Grenier. She considered the difference between his situation and Christy's and there was hardly any, beyond the certainty. It was easy to die in action. It was the dying in inaction that was so terrible. It was terrible for the women who were withheld, who had to remain. Take Cicely and Kathleen . . . frustrated girls. She felt safer about Kathleen, knowing how she would face tragedy. But for Cicely she had no assurance. She was female. She was meant to bear children. Kathleen would transpose the creative instinct. She would make something out of her own bitterness. Cicely would not transcend it in the same way. She hoped that she would marry; that in years to come she would meet some man, become a mother. And then she thought that she could wish her no bitterer wish.

She understood the wisdom of Mahomet when he offered a heaven without mothers. Through them death came, and birth, and death again. From youth one went down into the trap. One went down into love to wake with one's face pressed against the tomb.

Christy, who was about to die, was the one amongst them who was going to have his life preserved. Die at the right moment. Even if he did not know it, the truth was infallible. Felon! Felon! Somebody had called him a felon. In the church this morning, drenched with the humility which comes only through love, she had been able to transpose the felony. She had lived to an age that knew how often the lovely and the ugly could turn over, how out of the night the day comes; and even the sunlight can make music out of the rust on iron bars.

Immediately you became sure of anything, good or evil, it rose and denied you.

The denial had happened too often. She would never live again.

She was startled as though caught in secret when, suddenly, without warning, she saw Cicely come down the stone stairs. Her face was pale and wet with tears.

'My poor child!' she cried.

Cicely stood, perplexed and stricken. She became ashamed and flustered, showing a deceit to Catherine which she would not otherwise have suspected. 'Oh! I came

. . . I had to come . . . I am sorry, but I did so want to see him alone.' She descended the few remaining stairs into Catherine's arms. Her sobs had nothing at all to do with her deceit.

Catherine knew. She put her arms round the shaking shoulders. 'My poor child,' she repeated, remembering Christy's shaved head. She let her sob herself into control.

She stood separate again, looking at Catherine with shamed eyes. 'Will you forgive me?'

'Forgive you for what? There is nothing. Do not tell me. You have seen him? You have seen that they have . . . cut his hair.'

'Yes! How did you know! Did Redmond tell you?'

'I saw him. I saw him very early this morning.'

'You saw him!'

The shame had become a challenge. 'Yes, Cicely. I, too, wanted to see him alone.'

The challenge expired. 'He never told me.'

It was as water on Catherine's burning soul when she said that. He had not told her. It had been too great to tell. 'There wasn't time . . .' she began.

'No! No!' Cicely denied her, 'we had no time to speak of anything outside . . . Oh! He would like to see a priest. I have promised that he shall see a priest.'

Outside, she thought; and her whole spirit stood within, close to him. 'That is a very good idea, Cicely. It will comfort him.'

'I am so glad. I thought you would object, I was sure that you would object.'

'No,' she said simply, 'why should I?' She looked at the girl with mercy, and beyond all limits.

'The others — Kathleen and Valentine, they will be sure to object. They will think that I have got hold of him.'

'No, Cicely, I do not think that they will think of it in that way. I do not think that they will object. They will accept it as his wish.'

'You really think that?'

'Yes,' she hoped it.

There was a pause. 'What are you going to do?'

'I,' said Catherine, 'I am going to stay here.'

'What for?'

She ignored the inquisitiveness. The girl dried her eyes
and put the tiny handkerchief back in her purse. 'I shall
wait until Kathleen comes. She has gone to Redmond's with
Valentine. She, also (she had to say it, and she said it
completely without malice) wants to see Christy.' The fact
that it was his last day, his last day perhaps in suspense,
arose and spread itself in their minds.

'May I stay with you?'

She made way for her on the stone bench. She was
indifferent to her again, scarcely aware of her.

'Do you think that they will let him see a priest?'

She was not certain who she meant. 'Who?'

'The prison people.'

'Why, of course. Of course. They will expect it.' They
would be very polite about it. They were even attached to
the prison. It struck her as absurd that they should have
clergymen attached to prisons, a ridiculous mockery, like
doctors for the dying. It was as though they were going to
transfer him into some prison in eternity. 'You must not
have the prison priest,' she said with a wildness in her voice
that made Cicely stare at her.

'But if they won't let him have any other. I should like
him to have a priest, a young priest from Saint Anastasia's.'

'From Saint Anastasia's,' she repeated, and was flooded
again with the image of Mary with her embalmed son on
her knees. 'We shall not be able to embalm him.' She saw
the fright in Cicely's eyes and assuaged her: 'Yes, that is a
very good idea, Cicely.'

The big bell clanged and the warder opened the great
doors to let in somebody who was not Kathleen. Catherine
saw his manner operate on a small, old man who had
brought a parcel tied up in a red handkerchief. She wanted
to jump up and go over and shake the warder and make
him let the man alone, let him go through, with his little
red-wrapped package which was so obviously an act of
love. Faith, hope and charity and acts of contritions. Oh,
leave him alone! Stop bullying him! her thoughts urged
with all her will to the warder. She got up and walked

towards him. Almost as though he felt her prayer he yielded. He had, she saw, meant to yield all along. He insisted, however on seeing the contents of the package, and shook out before their eyes a woman's cotton chemise and a pair of flannelette knickers, and a pair of fawn, cheap stockings. The old man held the knotted handkerchief in his hand. The warder rammed the clothes back into the old man's grasp. 'And what's this?' he demanded, and peered into the red knotted handkerchief. He took out from it a tiny bunch of late nasturtiums, yellow and red as flames. Catherine caught her breath. A hand pushed up from earth holding the burning bright flowers. The prison became a tomb, cold stone, and remote. The flowers burned there like sunshine through a hole in darkness.

'She loves them,' the old man was saying.

'They are lovely,' Catherine answered him and knew that she would never see them separate from him again. In any garden he would be there with this trembling devotion in his eyes.

The warder directed him down the corridor and through the stone archway. He watched him go, turned to Catherine: 'Murdered her infant!'

Catherine closed her eyes against him. A sigh escaped her, a flame as the flowers had been.

Cicely shuddered. She was upset, not by pity for the man, not because like Catherine she had been caught in another human being's emotions, but by the brutality of the warder's revelation.

The bell clanged again and this time it was Kathleen. 'I hurried. I did not want to keep you waiting, Mother.'

'Thank you, but I have been waiting. I came too soon. Cicely has just seen him.'

'Already!'

'Yes,' the challenge was there again. And it wasn't necessary, for Kathleen's manner was very gentle with her. 'Is he . . . well, Cicely? Mother said he was cheerful.'

Always that little stop before the adverb. And she had not said that he was cheerful.

'He wants,' said Cicely, 'to see a priest!' the look she gave

Kathleen was defiant.

Kathleen measured it and maintained her gentleness, her sympathy. 'That must comfort you, a little, you are glad because he wants to see a priest.'

'Yes, I am glad.' The opposition died out of her and she went flat like a balloon, crumpled, deprived of something that was supporting her.

They all stood, for seconds only, feeling this emptiness. It made Kathleen impatient: 'I am going up. Will you still wait for me, Mother? Good-bye, Cicely, I hope that you will find your priest, it will be a link for you.'

Cicely said, as she disappeared up the stairs, turning to Catherine: 'Would you like me to stay with you?'

Catherine knew quite well that it wasn't to stay with her, but to be there when Kathleen descended again. 'If you want to.' Thought and action were muted, muffled for her, attendant. She could not blame Cicely nor even judge her. It had been like that with Mitchell. And then suddenly, with Mitchell, it had ended and the music had come full-blown and perfect. She swung out between miracle and madness. Was it not queer that in contact with this absurd girl who loved her son she could so distinctly recall the triumphant music of Mitchell? It was the nasturtiums and the 'murdered her infant.' She had stood in the garden with Mitchell and for the first time known what it was to desire a child. Understood. The trumpets of the petunias were open wide and blown with bees. The trumpets of the nasturtiums were as bright and brittle and brassy as flames. The sunshine had gone away and the grey stone walls of the gaol corridor looked as though nothing could ever be written on them. The record was done on the living beings who ran, calligraphic, to and fro between the grey walls. She had desired Mitchell's child and she had borne another man's. So would this girl.

She looked at her, not stealthily but deliberately. She was sitting close to her on the bench. She ought not to have worn a grey dress. Why, oh why! exclaimed Catherine to herself, does she wear a grey dress here? It makes her one with the walls, cinerates her. She is like that dead town in the Alpilles which has taken on the colour of the rocks on which it is perched.

'I hope that you do not really mind about Christy asking to see a priest.'

She was back on it as though it gave her pleasure. She put her hand on the girl's knee and said firmly but not loudly: 'I am, on the contrary, glad. I quite understand why he should have asked.'

'I suggested it . . . but he was speaking as though he wanted me to suggest it.'

'Exactly.'

The silence that fell was not, this time, of her making. They waited for Kathleen. There was nothing but this waiting. They had been waiting for days. And when she tried to catch the time before they had begun to wait it seemed more than one life-time ago. Waiting was like a needle that ran you through a thousand patterns and colours. One became a tiny thread, pulled hither and thither. 'Waiting is a sort of death.'

For the first time that morning Cicely's voice had a note of unity in it, of appeasement: 'She will come, she will come soon.' She came even as she spoke.

Like Cicely, Kathleen's face was wet with tears. She descended upon them in thunder and lightning; sweeping them up and along with her: 'Come along, come out of this, come!' And to the warder she said: 'Open the door quick.' Out in the street she stood with her hands pressed on her breast, breathing hard.

Catherine felt old, and cold, full of strange strength. She put her arm through her daughter's: 'Kathy! Don't take it like that.'

'Oh! Mother, there isn't any hope! There isn't any! I know! I feel it! I feel as though he were being flung away! They don't deserve him. Oh! why did he? What does it mean?'

'He knows why he did it and for what cause,' Cicely declared stubbornly.

'He doesn't! He has just said to me that he doesn't know why it should have happened.'

'You are confusing his meaning. He means that he

doesn't know why it should happen like this.'

'You cannot think for him. You can only think your own thoughts. He knows. He said . . . the blood that has gone into this earth. Oh! Mother, if I could tear him out of it!' She wheeled upon Cicely who was a pace or two behind: 'Why don't you rescue him between you? If you cared . . .'

'We do care!' she cried, being loyal.

'He is flung away . . . the way you fling dust! A sow that eats her own farrow . . . .'

Cicely came level with them. There were two pink spots in her cheeks. 'Don't you dare . . .'

Catherine went between them. 'Don't quarrel! Kathy! Do mind what you are saying.'

'I don't care whether she understands or not. She doesn't understand. She's just an idealist, stupid . . . .'

'I do understand.'

Catherine, between them, stopped walking. 'I can't stand this. You must not expect me to. There! Go on without me.'

Neither of them went on. Kathleen said: 'I am not going to leave you. Valentine said I wasn't to leave you.'

'I'm not a child.'

'I,' said Cicely, 'I will go on and get the priest.'

'Be sure to get one who . . . understands your ideals,' Kathleen remarked with real bitterness, and strained the bitterness into apology. 'Don't mind me, don't mind what I am saying. I am crazy. It is all terrible to me . . . too terrible . . . .'

'And don't you think it is terrible for me?' Cicely retorted and was defeated more by Kathleen's answer.

Kathleen took her suddenly in her arms. 'Of course it is. I know it is. Oh! It isn't only Christy . . . there go! Go and get your priest.'

Without a word Cicely walked ahead of them. Her arm swung and her grey legs looked very firm and determined, and knowing where they were going to, above her high heels. Catherine noticed that the heels were a trifle to high for her. She was mute, without rebuke, prepared to let Kathleen exhaust her.

'She is stupid, Mother. She thinks as though she were the only one. Why, he has been with us all his life!'

'All his life.'

The tone of her voice stopped the torrent in Kathleen.
'Mother!'

And after that they walked on without speaking. They
passed the church, the newspaper man at the park railings.
They came to the hotel.

'Here we are.'

Catherine came to a dead stop: 'This is the hotel.'

'Yes, Mother, don't you see that it is the hotel?'

'I see. I cannot, I do not want to go in. There is only that
room with all those people, and the bedrooms, and the strip
of pile carpet down to the bathroom. No, Kathy, I can't. I
can't stand it.'

Kathleen's voice took on the same note of unity, wiping
away the opposition, that she had heard in Cicely's: 'But
where, where would you like to go to? There is nowhere.
Would you like to go out to Gorabbey? Shall we go out
there, together, mother? Would you like to?'

'No. Not Gorabbey.' She saw the speckled laurels, the
dark deflowered rhododendrons in the park opposite. 'Let
us go into the park, we will find a seat there.' It had come to
that. She had nowhere to go. If Kathleen had not been with
her she might have gone into the church. But not with
Kathleen, nor after Cicely.

They crossed the street into the wide, gravelled paths of
the park. A flock of Indian ducks were sporting in the
water, and the martins were playing their skimming game,
dipping and flying over the low tranquil water and rising
with their beaks full. The swans were on the island, shut
into a hollied safety. Willows and limes excluded them, and
the willows even hung over and made arcades for them in
the green stagnant water. There was a scent of balsam in the
air. It was still the morning. She found it hard to believe that
it was still the morning and the day had yet to follow. The
sun had gone and clouds were massed and thickened in the
sky. All sorts of people were fluttering like the birds in the
park. She took no notice of them, no less, than of the birds,
the little busy birds.

They sat on an isolated seat in front of the lake. The scent was not balsam, it was like that Asiatic snowdrop plant whose name she could not remember. It had white flowers and a hot sharp taste.

'Mother!' Kathleen was sitting upright and tense beside her. 'I could not help it. That girl gets on my nerves. She's so full of conclusions, and this morning . . . after Dédé and Christy . . .'

Catherine's hand went down on hers.

'And they have shaved him! What does that mean?'

'It may not mean anything.'

'I have no hope now, none. Valentine is the only one, and I suppose Cicely.'

'I do not think that Cicely is thinking of him with any element of hope.' She had to be fair to her. The girl only wanted to serve him.

'I have no hope.'

She could find no words with which to meet this declaration. She had not cheated herself with any hope. It made it more terrible for those who had.

'Unless they rescue him. They have rescued others who were proved to be guilty. Valentine is convinced beyond all argument of his innocence.'

'Let us not talk about it.' It was a plea from her soul. 'It can do no good.'

'I'll try not to.' And immediately she continued, pushing the words as though she could plug her resolve with them: 'Redmond says we must go on collecting for him, that we are not to stop. They have already got enough signatures to move a whole government, if you can convince by numbers.'

The last word went on and on, numbers. Deuteronomy. Numbers. Leviticus.

'But now, since I have seen him I cannot. I should be so afraid of losing my temper. Oh! Mother, I feel that I want to scream out: Why have they shaved him? What does it mean?'

Catherine sighed deeply. Her mind again repeated the last word. Mean?

And, abruptly, Kathleen stopped. There were no people,

no footsteps, only themselves and the flying, swooping, heedless martins. The stillness was healing, winding them as fine gauze over a wound. Into it there came the long, distant roar of the trams, and bell-notes falling like bird-notes. And in the trees behind them a thrush thrilled out its passion. The song ceased and the stillness came again. Rain fell, large well-spaced drops, and the air took on a sharp voyaging wind.

Kathleen stood up: 'We must go in. We cannot stay here in the rain.'

'But not to the hotel.'

'Then where!'

She looked at her and saw how it troubled her. It was for this that Valentine had told her not to leave her. Valentine was at Redmond's. 'Let us go to Redmond's. I am sure that he will let me wait there.' There! She had revealed her suspense. 'Is Valentine there?'

'He was there when I left him.'

The rain had quickened and closened and was falling in earnest. She thought that Cicely would be drenched in her light dress. Kathleen was safe in her sensible coat and skirt and she herself had put on her old coat, the brown one that she had had for years and that had been torn the night that she had spent in the woods at Gorabbey, the night that she had not slept. Years ago, ages ago. She had passed through so many worlds since then. She had come into this world where Cicely and Kathleen disputed and Christy's head was shaved, and the man had published the article. And where the church was in everybody's hands. She saw distinctly as she passed through the open gates, the picture of Saint Brigid with the church in her hands, the church of life.

She had had no occasion to tell Christy that soon he would be able to look down upon the little church of her life which she held in her hands.

Kathleen hailed a cab and they got into it. That was the first cab for the day. Hotels and cabs, the street, the gaol, the public park.

Valentine had not yet left. Catherine was aware that his

mood had changed. He was worried and impatient. He ought not to have read all those newspapers, or discussed them with Redmond. Redmond was very gentle with her, he had not forgotten their conversation. It linked him to her so that she could sit quiet and patient amongst the people there — Kathleen and Valentine and the confidential clerk and the stenographer who still held his pad and pencil. They were in continual movement so that the pattern of their grouping was always changing; first Kathleen and Valentine by the window, then Valentine; stooped, leaning on his hands, over papers on Redmond's table; and then Kathleen in the deep chair beside Redmond reading a letter. She looked up from the letter and said angrily to Valentine: 'I wish to heavens they (the 'they' of the letter) would rescue him!'

Valentine was furious when she said that: 'Don't be a fool!' He said it as he would have said it to Cicely.

'Here it seems advisable to be a fool, to take fool risks!' she retorted. Catherine was thankful that she did not quote Joyce.

Valentine walked up and down the room after that in quick strides, making a semi-circular sweep with his outer leg when he came to the turns. As he came towards her he seemed to rise like a giant and as he went away again she saw him as his normal self. He was taller than any of them. Redmond asked her if she would like to read any of these letters and papers that they were discussing and she answered 'no.' What was the use? He looked significantly at Valentine when she said that and Valentine approved. Kathleen pretended not to hear. But she heard quite well.

They were preserving her. She was willing to help them to carry on the preservation by not wanting to see anything, hear anything. How could they guess how far beyond all preservation she was! While she was thinking this she had a piercing premonition that Cicely was on the way, that she was coming and that they would quarrel again. It braced her. She sat up, prepared, and praying for her wits to be strong. She was right. Cicely came into the room. She went direct to Redmond, pleading in her rather sweet thin voice:

'Please, Mr Redmond, Father Ignatius wants to see Christy, can you arrange it?'

'In the name of God, what for?' Valentine bellowed.

His voice roared against Catherine's ears in its suddenness and was magnified a hundredfold. The girl turned towards him and stared with her mouth slightly open. There was a queer strayed smirk on Kathleen's lips.

Redmond seemed to screw up like a violin string. 'Has he asked to see Father Ignatius or have you arranged it?'

'He asked to see a priest.'

'A priest or did he say clergyman?' Valentine demanded.

Her answer to him was as straight as to Redmond: 'He asked to see a priest, a catholic priest.'

She had no air of triumph but Valentine took it as though she had, in some intangible way, scored against him, beaten him. His arms flopped like broken pinions and he turned to Kathleen as though, in this, they were allied. It was, perhaps, that that made her say:

'It is strange, Cicely, but when I saw him, after you saw him, he never mentioned it.'

'We spoke of . . .' she hesitated, and found the definition, 'of preparation for death, of being ready, whether he needed to or not. It was special . . . .'

And Catherine, listening, seeing their anger, thought: he gave the fruit to her, Cicely, who was hiding it as though she had stolen a pearl, hiding it beneath her admission, beneath that word special. The tree was not Cicely's. And it was pearled with fruit. She seemed, to herself, to rise out of the tree when she said, calming them all: 'It is quite natural that he should wish to see a stranger . . . .'

'But a strange creed!' Valentine protested.

She looked at Redmond who was a catholic, to save Valentine, and she reasoned: 'Is any creed strange at a time like this? Any spiritual comfort? Your Grandfather, or even Mitchell, would have been likely to do the same thing.'

She saw them steady back into the family attitude. Kathleen sealed it: 'If it is his wish, it is his wish.'

Cicely was looking a little like an apostle, and Redmond full of tact was dictating a final phrase to his typist.

Valentine plunged a shaft into Cicely: 'I wish to God, Cicely, you could control your manner of owning him. You're not the only one.'

'Poor Cicely!' Catherine said and put out a hand towards her. She was strangely rewarded by the girl's smile. And she was grateful for the way she said to Valentine:

'I can't help it, Valentine. I know, but I can't help it. I suppose it is always like that.'

Her words had an effect on him. Catherine saw him take them in and turn them over and be stirred by them. 'I suppose so. I hope not,' and after a thoughtful second, 'forgive me if I'm a brute. We're all on edge this morning.'

Redmond chimed in then, taking Cicely away from Valentine's attention. 'This collection must go on. There must be no break or they will say that something has really been found out. The only way to kill this spy story is by ignoring it.'

'I am quite willing,' she replied. 'I'll go at once.'

She acted like a spur upon them. Kathleen stood up and also said: 'I am willing. I do not think that it is of any use only on that score, on the score of tactics.'

'But that is very important,' Redmond declared.

Valentine agreed. 'Yes, it is best to change nothing.' He looked at Catherine as if she was, in some fashion, in his way. He was wondering what to do with her.

'I shall stay here, if Mr Redmond will let me?'

'But, of course, you are very welcome.'

His words came warm and frank but his eyes were troubled. He did not really want her to stay. She had nowhere else to go. 'I could address envelopes for you.'

Valentine was shocked. He racked his wits and found a solution: 'Look here, Mother! It must be about time that you had something to eat. You were up so early? Did you sleep well?'

'I slept the whole night through.' Kathleen had found her in her day clothes.

'Good! And you are quite ready for some lunch?'

'What time is it?' He looked at his wrist-watch and told her that it was on the tick of eleven. Kathleen came over and

kissed her. It was so odd to be kissed by Kathleen and to be
having lunch at eleven and not to know where you were
going to have it. Cicely came and put her lips against her
cheek. She was paralysed. The astonishment stayed in her
mind and took a great effort to move it. Intimacies where no
intimacies should be. The dislodgement shook her, made
her tremble, and the paralysis went. Valentine looked as
though he, too, were going to lean over her and touch her
cheek. The door shut behind Cicely and Kathleen. She stood
up.

'But isn't it much too early for you, Valentine?'

'No, it is not too early.'

She liked Redmond, liked the way he held out his hand
and the expression in his eyes. She knew that she did not
want to ask before Valentine but she asked all the same:
'And the Home Secretary?'

'Not a word, not a word yet.'

Valentine put his hand on her shoulder. She went with
him. There was a great crowd of people round the door.
There had not been a crowd when she came in, a few people
perhaps, not enough to notice, but this was truly a crowd.
She clutched Valentine's arm and he rushed her into a cab
that was waiting and told the man where to drive. 'But it
may be waiting for somebody else,' she protested, 'do ask
him.'

'What does it matter?' Valentine snapped down the
blind.

She asked him herself, tapping on the glass until he
turned. 'Were you free?'

'I was engaged for you, for an old lady and a dark
gentleman, a young lady engaged me to wait here until you
came out.'

That was Kathleen. She was moved, shaken, by such
thoughtfulness.

'Trust Kathleen's brains,' Valentine said in her ear and
saved her.

She lay back against the saggy leather. What did that
crowd mean. 'Is it always like that . . . such a crowd?'

'Not quite so many. They mean nothing, mother. Idlers

who read the papers in the public library.'

Idlers who read the morning papers. It was only a phrase to her. Valentine was speaking figuratively. They were not there because they were idlers. They were there because of the spectacle. Seeing them made her unreal to herself. It was all a play, and it would pass. Instantly she knew she was cheating herself and that it was no play. Afterwards she would understand it better.

And then she was pierced and stabbed into the present and she had an overwhelming desire for her son Christy. It was such an overpowering hunger that she cried out for him, seizing Valentine as though he were doing something to thwart her: 'I want Christy, to see him. Can we not go there now. I feel that he needs me, needs me at this moment. He needs me! He may be ill.'

He put his arm round her: 'No, Mother, he is not ill. I will take you to him . . . later, after we have lunch.'

'No! Now!' He thought that she was hysterical. She was quite sane, over-sane, clairvoyant. This need was imperative. There was no denying it.

'But I know that Redmond was going down to see him, he was going immediately after we left him. Do take my advice, Mother! They would not let you see him again so soon.'

That appeared true to her. She had seen him such a little while ago. As she thought of it it came back as though it had only been a moment ago. He had said — I am not afraid. I just do not want to go out like that — and he had snapped his fingers like Valentine. My son! she prayed to him with burning thoughts; it will not be death. It will not. It will capture life for you so that death will never be able to touch you. Valentine was speaking:

'You must keep steady, Mother! Where should we be without you?'

It was not visibly that she was of use to them, as he meant. It was in her soul. They were all there: Christy and Kathleen and Dédé and Cicely and even Valentine who was a rock of sense. They were in her soul as in a rock. They were the miraculous roses in the rock of her soul.

It was the same as yesterday. They went to the same place. They had the same table behind the screen. They had coffee afterwards in tiny green bordered cups. She ate what came but without tasting it. The food was Tartarean food to her.

When there was nothing more left to linger over, Valentine got up. She got up too, took her bag out of the space between the back and seat cushion in the leather covered seat. Valentine said: 'Sit down, Mother, I am going to telephone.' She sat down and waited. The waiting would never end. It went from one wait to another.

He came back in a few moments. 'I've telephoned to the garage to bring round the car. I am going to take you for a run into the country.'

His voice was thick with determination. Nevertheless she asserted her own will. 'But what about Christy? I wish to see him.'

'You can't, just yet.'

She would not be broken. 'I must see him, Valentine.'

'I will bring you back to him. This run will do you the world of good.'

'Not to Gorabbey.'

He assessed her motive. 'Not if you don't wish to.'

'No,' she was immutable, 'I could not bear it,' only in the night, in the nightly darkness.

'Then! Where shall I take you?'

'Valentine . . . do not ask me!' She surrendered. She bore his tenderness, his touching hands, as he tucked a rug behind her as she liked. The rain had stopped and the air when the wind missed it was hot and thunderous. The movement of the car eased her because it was not going to stop for ages — no hotel or gaol or lawyer's door to arrest it. And when they began to run through the countryside by a road, on which the rain had laid the dust, between brightly washed fields, through fields bereft and harvested, she realised that Valentine had been right. She had needed this. It brought everything into its right place. The air wiped her as it wiped the fields. She knew where she was again and that Christy had been condemned. The paralysing numbness abated and her mind moved out again from all their nerves-on-edge. She was able to see through the tangle of Kathleen and Cicely and Valentine and pull them out like threads. They quarrelled because they were defeated. They had done their best. She was the only one amongst them who was not defeated because she had never allowed her soul out of its place in Christy's fate. His death had been there, for her, from the moment of his condemnation. Her flights had been circumscribed by it. She had never reached beyond him.

Valentine had taken the road out along the Bay, so that they were running now between the villas perched on the slope of the hills and the spread blue water. The clouds were all swept west and the sky over the Bay was a deep indigo with thunder behind it, heavy, ready for shadow. There was a storm coming. It was odd how she could appreciate this world which was offered in such appealing guile and at the same time every sense in her body was beating in a rhythm that had turned from it. Valentine turned and smiled at her. His smile fixed him there like a snapshot taken on the low road at the edge of the bay. Hundreds of years later she would see that smile, greet it with recognition. His kindness was very deep in him but remote to her. She saw and felt it outwardly. They were going round a point by a high wall that enclosed a park; a lichened, crusted wall with alert amaranthine flowers springing out of it at intervals, when he brought the car to a stop. It was a lonely place, isolated, and safe against the lovely wall. Far, on the other side of the Bay a white envelope of a boat was sailing. You learned how to make them when you were a child: somebody leaning over the breakfast table and turning an envelope into the proper shape for you and you went out and sailed it in the swollen rainy stream, and Nurse said if it gets past the twigs (which were tacking the current) you will get what you wish for. She never got what she wished for.

'It is lovely here.'

'Beautiful,' she answered. She noticed that he had got thinner, she noticed it when he smiled and his lips went wider. He was like Luke when he was thinner. His arm lay along the seat in front of her and the metacarpal bones shone finely in his brown hand. Distant and softly as skirts passing, the skirts of nuns, she heard the waves of the bay break on the white sands. Between the rocks on the point above which they were arrested, the water was stained in a deep green from the shadow of the carrageen that floated in it. It was a beautiful world and it broke the heart. Every living thing died in it.

'Don't you feel better already?'

'Yes, I feel better.' Question and answer! Mere breaths on the brassy breast of the earth.

'I say, Mother, does it worry you, this about Cicely, about the priest?'

'Why should it? No.'

'She's more than I can stand sometimes.' He made a grimace.

'Yes, I see that. Kathleen is nicer to her than you. That is a little strange because Kathleen is a woman and Cicely is a woman too.'

'Kathleen is splendid . . . .'

'Yes.' She brought her eyes sharply into his. He wanted to tell her something — something about Kathleen. 'Kathleen is more forbearing than you because she is unhappy, unhappier than you, because of something personal as well as Christy.' She wished to let him know that she knew, that there was no need to tell her.

'I thought there was something. That Grenier chap?'

'Yes. It is nothing now. It is finished.' She meant nothing to tell him. It would never be finished for Kathleen.

'I can understand . . . thoroughly . . . .'

It was something about himself that he was going to tell her, not about Kathleen. She waited. Below the force of that 'thoroughly' there was trouble. He was unhappy. She could not ask him to tell her. She did not want to hear, she had no curiosity. But if he wanted to tell her it would perhaps help him to know that she understood. There was nothing left that her understanding could not stretch to, nothing.

He turned his head away and his other hand went to the

wheel. He evidently changed his intention. He told her
nothing. They slid round the headed road into the window
blowing from the east. No more was said between them,
until, about half an hour later, he asked her if she would like
to go back.

He took her to the gaol door. It was when he had
descended and was about to open the door for her, his hand
on it, that reserve peeled from him and he showed what he
had been hiding. 'Mother . . . you are so brave.'

'Well!' she waited.

I wish I could carry it off as well as you. You are an
example.'

She put her hand out on his to encourage him.

'Redmond . . . we didn't like to tell you until the last
moment, he sent off the signed petition yesterday . . . .'

He was watching her so vigilantly to see how she would
stand it.

'And last night . . . we telegraphed to the Home
Secretary.'

He came to a full stop and her mind came to a full stop
with him. At last she said: 'That means that we shall hear
very soon.'

'Very soon.'

'We thought wiser to rush it.'

She could say nothing to that. Time had no meaning from
her. She kept a measure that was beyond the mere passing
of days, or hours. He opened the door and they went into
the gaol together. She entered as she might have entered a
church, the same sense of Presence, of Being surrounded
her. Romeo and Juliet were enfolded in the tomb for her.
Tears were of no avail in these walls even if she had been in
a state to shed them. She was upheld and strengthened by
grief, by love, for there is no grief without love. And she
was repeating to herself as though she had seen it written
on the walls as a motto; this is the first time that I have been
here with Valentine. It had the significance of first
happenings. At last she said it aloud. 'This is the first time
that I have been here with you.'

Immediately he took it as an opportunity: 'Will you let

me run up to see him first?'

'If you have anything to say to him that you do not want me to hear do go up first and tell him.'

She watched him bound up the stiff stairs. He came down again in a few minutes. His face was stricken. 'They have shaved him!'

'Yes, I know.' Not one of them had said that his hair had been cut. It was when she had seen him in that cell first, after his sentence, that she had known from the movement of his hand in his hair, that he was not ready to die. He didn't want to go out like that. He had snapped his fingers.

She went first up the stairs. This time she did not keep her eyes on the heels ot the warder. She looked straight ahead ready to catch the first glimpse of Christy. He was waiting for her. He knew she was coming. Along the straight walls she was conscious, before she saw him, of his form pressed against the grill. His voice greeted her:

'Mother! Dear Mother!'

He hands shut quickly as though over a gift. She heard it echo and re-echo through her being: Mother, dear Mother. Generations flocked in it. It was a homing cry, a cry of ages. When she reached him they stood, the three of them, without saying a word, beyond speech. Christy came out of the moment first. The words fell hot from his heart as though they were suffocating him:

'I would like to be able to take you into my arms, to comfort you.'

She smiled at him as one who said — I am beyond comfort.

Valentine comforted her: 'Mind you, we have no news yet!'

She took a deep breath. She trusted Redmond again. 'We, Valentine and I have been into the country, Christy. It . . .' she rewarded Valentine, 'has saved me from breaking down. I shall not break down . . .' she comforted Christy, 'if I did I should be of no use to you!'

'But yes,' he protested, 'you are always of use. I feel . . . it is strange how I feel you near me. When you are not there you are, I feel, there all the time.'

'I am.' In two words she hid her secret, hid it from

Valentine the witness. It was not hidden from Christy for he drew his strength from it.

Valentine took another advantage. He said before her, making her the witness: 'Christy . . . you never did it?'

Christy gave him a resolute unflinching look, glanced from warder to warder and back again. 'I was guilty.'

Valentine's hands fell, heavy as stones, into his pockets. 'It is a queer thing to happen to us.'

Christy weighed what he wanted to say and gave the skimming: 'If only you could bring yourself to see it from another angle. If you could bring yourself, for instance, Val, to see me as a common murderer, you might, because you know that I am not a common murderer, see me as I am.'

Valerie was silent. In the circumstances he knew, they each knew, that words would take root and last forever.

'Cicely was getting you a priest, a priest from Saint Anastasia's, Christy. Has he come?

'No, not yet.'

She had asked it to save him from Valentine. 'Wasn't it queer . . . from Saint Anastasia's.'

'It did not seem queer to me, just right.'

Valentine was mystified: 'Did you know, Mother? I thought Cicely did it on her own.'

It could not be explained to him, yet she did not want him to be mystified. 'We each had similar thoughts. It was a coincidence that I went into Saint Anastasia's this morning early, in passing.'

'Did you want a priest?' Valentine asked.

'Yes,' he nodded.

Question and answer. The bare, bare surface. It might have been a railway train and Christy leaning out to say good-bye. The little clipped closed sentences of separation. This meant departure. And suddenly she was suffocated, hating it with all her being. All the separations of her life gathered and fulfilled a climax. She was scattered again and lost. The warder was interfering and Valentine was resenting it; and Christy's eyes had the same look as Teazle's when he wasn't being taken. She had a wild choking longing to reach through the bars and take him into

her arms as Mary had taken her son; to hold him close to
her as she had held him when he was an infant, a small
umbilical infant out of his bath. Her breasts were dry now.
It was a long time since he had been born. He was a solid
young man in front of her, behind bars. They were speaking
quickly in a rhythm against the warder's interference.

'If there is a telegram Redmond will be coming to see you
again to-day.'

'They've been quite sports about my visits, haven't they?'
Christy's voice was too cheerful.

'I should think so! Redmond fixed that up. He had stood
by you.'

'Magnificently.'

She was grateful when Valentine, his arm through hers,
pulled her away. It was beyond her own volition. Christy
had not said good-bye, but au revoir. They went down the
stairs together, Valentine's arm still supporting her. She
was glad of it. The heaviness was in her again, the loaded
physical tiredness in her nerves and body that stifled her
spirit. She would arise again from it directly. She knew now
truly where she was and that this would pass.

She sat by Valentine in the car, and shut her eyes against
the streets and multitudes; the grey gloomy street of the
prison and then the sordid poverty of the mixed shops —
the jeweller's, which was always a pawn-broker's; the shop
with the cheap pinafores; the oily slab of the fishmonger's;
the women with Life written large in their faces; the sharp
bright-eyed skinniness of the children. The car skimmed
past them, past the old fine debased streets into streets that
showed green in front-gardens. Where was he taking her?
She did not ask. He brought the car to a standstill before a
suburban sweet shop and restaurant. She thought that he
was getting out to buy cigarettes, but he waited for her:

'Here's a tea-shop, Mother, away from everything. I am
going to give you some tea.'

Again she had to force herself to recognise his
thoughtfulness, to smile at him.

They sat at a little glass-topped and brass-rimmed table
under a red striped awning. Somewhere, over low

two-storeyed houses, tree-tops made a minute forest.

'Mother. I am proud of you.'

He had no need to be. She had her moments like the rest of them.

A woman bought their tea which had slopped on the tray, over the mineral waters address. She laid the table very carefully but with the plates on the wrong side.

Valentine poured out the tea: 'This . . . you know, Mother, it cannot last.'

It would end. She took the cup he was sliding towards her. With premeditation she said: 'I shall go away afterwards. I could not go to Gorabbey.' She could not go back into the world where they had friends and familiar, normal people. In the space of a few days' time she had disappeared from that world. She was in a world of hotels and gaols and . . . she gave the place a glance, this.

'But we cannot shut it up . . . not completely. It has to be kept heated.'

She knew that quite well. It was a house that pined and perished when left alone. 'I hope that you will live there as much as possible . . . if you want to.' Kathleen might not want to go back to Paris. When she said that to him she started as though she had probed him.

'I don't know . . . .'

'Not if you do not want to.' She released him.

'It isn't that.'

She did not wish it to continue. Could he not leave it? There was no need to talk about it just then. It could wait.

'The fact is, Mother, I feel I ought to marry.'

'I have always hoped that you would, that you all would.'

'I mean . . . pretty soon.'

She looked at him and read him to the depths. She knew what was coming so that when it came she was already frozen to meet it.

'There is a girl . . .' he hesitated and chose candour, 'a girl, well, not of our class. I must marry her.' He expected her silence and ran over it. 'Not because I have, as they put it, got her into trouble. But because, to be honest with you,

Mother, and because I want you to understand, I do not think that anything more genuine will ever come into my life.'

'Ah. She loves you? Or is it, Valentine, that she makes you love her?' It was not her experience that men were captured by great feminine love, but by their own love.

'Before this . . .' he made a vague gesture, 'I might not have done this. But now . . . .'

She touched his hand: 'If you feel that it is real, if it is real!'

'It is. She has been wonderful . . . .'

He had gone to her with his confidences. That was why she had had none, until now. Neither had she given any, nor had she demanded any. From him and Kathleen she suffered again separation. It was natural; she was the source, they were the streams, far from her. Solitary, she turned towards him and he mistook the sadness in her eyes.

'Mother! I told you now because I felt that it would not make any difference now . . . what I did. I am sorry if it grieves you.'

His reasoning was a little beyond her. 'I always care what happens to you. I hope that it will turn out happy.' She saw this girl moving from the house she had never seen in Windyharbour into Gorabbey. She loved Gorabbey. When she had said that she could not bear to go back there she had meant to desert the house, and not the house was deserting her. An unknown girl was going into possession; to be her son's bride and breed another generation; to bring strong, thoughtless blood into the race that treasured the Black Poems.

'I wish I could make you realise, without any blame to Christy, how he has, this affair, has made me see this.'

In his terror he had seized the first thing that seemed stable. She understood perfectly. She, herself, had been able to seize nothing. Nevertheless, apart from her acceptance of all that he was telling her, Gorabbey became part of the heartbreak she was enduring. Until this moment it had been preserved and left alone in the possession of all that was past. Now the future claimed and marked it with this event.

Her spirit rose to console it as though it was not a house but an organic being and of her own race. 'Listen, Valentine, what time is it?' Her voice was excited, quicker than she meant it to be.

'About three . . .' He looked at his watch.

'Only three!'

'We began the day early. Lunch at eleven.'

'Yes. Yes. Do you think that we have time to run out to Gorabbey?'

He stared at her until the stare softened into all that had made him ask Kathleen not to leave her. 'You want to go there now?'

'Yes, now,' he thought that she was unbalanced. This last blow, for he knew it was a blow, had brought her madness. She had to reassure him. 'I am quite sane, Valentine, only I have changed my mind.' It was a blow, but it resembled a blow that had fallen long ago and was only repeating itself. She knew all its effects.

'Don't fret about this, my marriage, Mother.'

She repeated: 'I hope you will be happy.'

He was busy with the gear. 'I shall have to pass the limit when I can, I want to be at Redmond's about six-thirty.'

There would be a telegram about 'six-thirty'. She sat back in the car, silent. The silence was a cloak to her. A telegram about six thirty! It beat into the burr of the car's speed: telegram — six-thirty. When Christy was a small boy and she had taken him on his first train, the slow station-stopping train into town that they had ceased to take since they had bought a car, she had made him listen to the rhythm. It started out: I — think — I — can — I — think — I — can, and quickened, between the stations, into I — thought — I — could — I — thought — I — could. They had kept it up for years.

She kept her eyes shut again going through the city but her thoughts she could not shut. All this had been built, built with hands: roads and bridges and prisons. Slave hands. She saw them magnified and gigantic against the stone walls of the prison, the dark brooding walls, slates on which only the secret and invisible could be written, put there by ugly distorted human hands. She had entered there for eternity. She took all criminals into the lap of her pity and enfolded them as though they, too, had sprung from her womb and were flesh of her own flesh. They were born into their criminal destiny as Hilary the Abbot had been born above the dark sea, and into its wonder. The wonder was always there, the fleece of mystery that could be wound by a turn of the hand. When it caught the sun life was life, and when it caught the shade life was death.

When they came to Windyharbour Valentine raced like mad. She was grateful although she knew that he was not doing it for her but for some obscure need of his own.

The familiar countryside was lovely to her — the golden reaped fields stencilled between the sea and far dim mountains. The white gables of the villages shining in the clear rainy air like a fleet of sails.

She saw the first larches of Gorabbey, stretched like fingers in greeting. In springtime there were acres of yellows, primroses and daffodils; the streams came down swollen from the hills; brown and muddied like all youth. In summer the air was shrill with the flights of young ravens. There was a month when the moles ran across one's feet in the evening roads and the sky was bright with flying stars and one wished . . . .

In winter there were fires in the rooms: the portraits came alive in the firelight. The archbishop always had a sudden smile of eternal redemption and Grandaunt Ahn (they never spelt the name Anne) enjoyed her joke. It was a house that said Peace! Peace! to its children. She hoped that it would bring that peace in earnest to Valentine's sons and daughters.

Peace! where there was no peace.

The beeches were already turned for autumn. They were the first to go.

They were running so quickly now that everything was a little blurred to her. In the village, when he slowed down by the school-house, Valentine gave the signal on his horn so that when they came to the gates Timothy had opened them and was standing there, rusty and crusty with age to greet them. Catherine smiled at him and blessed and thanked him in her heart for his long service. After this day she would never see him again.

She said to Valentine when they were out of sight, 'Let us get out here. I do not want to go into the house, only to go up to the Abbot's room and look out of the window.'

'Mother!' he was frightened. He did not trust her. 'I am coming, may I come with you?'

'Of course you may come.' She did not want him, but it made no difference.

They turned out of the scrunching gravel and out across the lawn. The geranium flames were still burning. And, by the Abbot's staircase the giant heliotrope was still stormed by butterflies. It brought Catherine's mind back to the span of days, back into the everyday world that she had outbounded. The key was in her pocket. She gave it to Valentine who mounted the steep steps in front of her.

This was farewell, good-bye. The house claimed it. It was as though she had meant to run away and it had known and had cried for her to come back. She was here. She was going, going everlastingly. She would never come back. Bodies had been carried out if it dead. Hers took leave of it alive. The death was within her.

She knew everything by heart. She only wanted to look through the windows as through the eyes. She went straight there and opened it and leaned out on her hands, and she felt that she could fall with the heaviness that was within her hear. Valentine was so close to her that he irritated her, close enough to catch her if she really fell. She drew herself in and putting her hands against him pushed him gently away from her.

'Don't be so afraid, Valentine . . . I am not that sort.'

The blood rushed up under his skin as though she had accused him of murder. He made no denial, none would come for him.

She turned away from him, sorry for him, but with no time to lose. This was very important to her, this drink of memory, this greeting, this hail and farewell of her soul going away. Going away from all associations into a state where she would never again make associations. She was done with this earth.

The nests lay in dark clots in the trees. In winter they were like black seals in the branches binding the pattern of the bare boughs. In the same frame the distant sea lay as in an Italian picture. She looked down on the land she had ridden through on Mitchell's horse and it seemed to her, as she looked, that her youth rode away from her there for ever. From China to Peru and round the world and out through the tiny gate of sleep . . . .

'There,' she turned to Valentine, 'it is finished.' It was a prayer said. She could get off her knees.

He came over and took her into his arms and held her, comforting her. She was an old woman and his mother and he held her as a lover would have held her, breathing his comforting love upon her, the protection of his young manhood. She was acutely aware of all that he would give the girl who was to take her place. She had a spring of pride in him, in his fine male body and dark face, the handsome face of all her people. But her blood did not answer him. She was ebb to his flow and in opposition. She was comfortless. Yet she raised her face to his and her lips met his. In her eyes, behind the sorrow that could not be hidden, was benediction, so that over and over again the grace she gave him would come back and strengthen him.

He did not know, of course, that in that moment she bestowed her worldly goods upon him; the house in which he was to make his home. He would come to know it years afterwards.

They went down again into the garden, past the heliotrope, and past the geranium-ringed fountain that burned like a sanctuary lamp.

'Keep those geraniums going,' she said.

'Everything will be taken care of.'

It was understood between them.

When they turned away from the gates she put the place away from her. She knew where she was going to. Her whole life had moved towards this hour.

She belonged to that communion of mothers who had

given their sons; whose sons have been taken.

All through that ride back to the city which enclosed the prison which enclosed her son, she sat upright; her hands closed and held down on either side of her. The ride was a moment to her, a moment of agony. She knew that there would be a telegram.

When they came to Redmond's door Valentine wanted her to wait in the car. She could not wait and went in with him.

He did not let her go through the door first. He went direct to Redmond's inner office, asking a clerk on the way if Redmond could see him. She shut the first door and watched his haste. It hurt her, not for herself, but for Christy. The clerk avoided her eyes. Suddenly she felt that she could not go into the inner office. They would have to come out to her. She thought of God's power and made no appeal to it. The leather on the clerk's desk was worn and the tooling was nearly invisible. His index finger-nail was full of ink. She remembered that Christy perspired continually in his cell, in the close air. It tired him out. In between his visits she could see him, hopeless, giving in physically, to the thick unnerving atmosphere. And then he would think of her, feel her near him and his soul would fill with courage . . . She held his head against her breast. Her spirit went out to him in great waves of light.

Redmond came out first. The telegram was in his hand. He held it out to her, dumbly, stupidly. She took it. She crumpled it into her hand. She could not, could not, read it. There was no need. Their silence told her.

She sat there, holding the telegram in her tightly closed hand. Valentine's eyes were unbearable. After long eternal seconds she spoke to them: 'When?'

Redmond answered her at last: 'To-morrow morning at eight o'clock.' At eight o'clock. She saw the gallows, the body swinging out. It was all over they said in a few seconds. She stood up. Everything was wiped out of her except this.

'When can I see him?'

It was again Redmond who answered, 'To-night.'

'To-morrow morning, too!'

'I am afraid not. I am afraid they will only let him see the priest to-morrow morning.'

The priest, the anointer. They would give her no embalmed body.

Suddenly Valentine collapsed into the chair against the wall at his side and shook with sobs. His deep bass sobs broke against her like storm. The clerk got up and went away. Redmond still stood, stupid. She could do nothing for Valentine. She could not rise to go to him. Her will did not wish to touch him. She could only bear her own sorrow. It was so great that she could not rise from under it to go to Valentine. She was glad when Redmond's stiff hand dropped on his shoulder, when he said words to him that had no meaning for her.

She waited. When Redmond turned to her, prepared at last for the solace that was trapped in such anguish she repelled him by her motionless. She sat so still that he did not dare to break against her.

It was she, herself, who stood up, who set him going. 'I ask but one thing . . .' she turned to Valentine, 'I ask it from you all. Let me be the last to see him . . . the last except the priest?'

Valentine came over to her. She put her hands out: 'Do not touch me!'

'But yes, Mother! You shall see him last!' He had an air of offering her heaven and earth, the sun and moon.

'Thank you.' She wished he would go away where she could not see his eyes, but she knew that she would be aware of them even if he turned his back on her. 'Where are the others?'

He turned and repeated her question to Redmond.

'They have gone down to the gaol, your sister and his girl together. Cicely wanted . . .' he gave a meaningful glance at her and continued, 'to see him first.'

'That, I quite understand.' She preserved the girl with sympathy.

'Come,' one of them said, 'let us go now.'

Once more she got into the grey car behind Valentine.

Redmond sat beside him. They arrived at the gaol with a strange sort of smoothness that was unreal to her. The same warder. The same stairs. The same bench on which she was to wait until they had each seen him. It was her wish and she had to bear its fulfilment. She asked the same question:

'Where are the others?'

Redmond went back to the door and spoke to the warders. Valentine went after him. They returned and said nothing.

'Well . . .' she said, 'tell me. You see how I am taking it. I am quite calm. You have nothing to be afraid of. I shall not break down.'

She inspired and relieved them. She saw it happen to them. They did not know that she was already broken, 'Cicely is with him . . . and your daughter too.'

'Together!'

'Yes, it seems that Cicely went first . . . that she would not leave him . . . .'

She had made a scene, and Kathleen had had to go. She felt sorry for Kathleen. 'Poor child!' she said, 'I know. I am glad Kathleen was here for her.' They would play it out against each other.

Redmond made her sit down on the bench. She had known all along. She knew now that she had known. It was not his death, but the manner of his dying. He was not ready. The Home Secretary saw no reason . . . No! No! The telegram was still tightly enclosed in her hand. She would read it sometime. 'Why,' she said quietly to Redmond, 'do you think they refused?' She gave another question to Valentine, 'to prove that he was not a spy?'

'They had to prove it.'

He was the payment.

She waited. Redmond went up the stairs and came down again. She gathered that he had already been and that he had returned to his office for her and Valentine. 'They could not have thought him guilty,' she diminished their excuse.

'That I can't tell you.'

The law was limited. She was clear about it, cold as though it was the aftermath. The aftermath, she knew would be more real. She sat there with a patience that counted only with eternity. She heard somebody coming down the stairs. It was Cicely and Kathleen. Her first thought was that Kathleen had not seen him alone, that she had been robbed. The look she gave Kathleen gave her this solace for she said in return for it:

'He asked me to stay with her, not to leave her. I have promised.' 'Poor child.' She made the effort to break before Cicely the coldness that she would not be able to fathom. She was prepared when the girl fell into her arms, on her knees. She gathered the poor sobbing form close and held it with the full consolation that she knew Christy expected. She could refuse him nothing. But she could not make her heart feel. She made a brave show of it.

And then Valentine, thinking of her more than of Cicely, pulled the girl on to her feet, and admonished her to be brave, to pray. Valentine the careless admonished her to pray. He knew that prayer would give her an outlet.

Kathleen sat on the bench with her arms rigid in front of her and her hands clenched.

'Kathy! Take her away. Take her to a church!' Valentine made a sign with a hand behind Cicely's shoulder that he wanted to go upstairs. 'Go on up, Redmond . . . do your best.' He motioned, with the same hand, Redmond before him.

Catherine did not dare to touch Kathleen, to say a word to her. She understood her too well. Nothing needed to be spoken between them.

Kathleen rose obediently and tried to draw Cicely away. 'Come! Come!'

'Yes, Cicely, go,' Catherine said, covering the child with love. She felt love for her in that instant. 'Go! Go to Saint Anastasia's.'

Kathleen and the sobbing, choking girl went out together. They went out through the doors for the last time. In the brief interval that the door was open a cry rose from the street, a cry from several people, a Barabbas cry. Too late. Catherine shuddered.

Valentine heard it too. 'The news has got round. They've been quick!'

And the crowd cried for Barabbas to be let off. Christ was hanged between two thieves. 'Will they be there when we go out?'

'Most likely. They will be there all night, I expect,' he answered her. He stood before her, stooping, his arms falling. Mercifully he did not put his hands on her. 'Well, Mother, I am going up . . . I shall tell him that you are here.'

'Yes,' she said, 'tell him.'

She waited. The corridor was full of the twilight, clouds had thickened out the sunset. Also it was always the morning sunlight which came here. The warder looked smaller. He looked — married, as though he did this to support a wife and family. He did not care. All this meant nothing to him. It meant nothing to the Home Secretary who had seen no reason why the sentence . . . .

Other mothers. Other women had suffered this. She had been born upon the earth to suffer this deep terrifying knowledge.

She did not know what day it was. Time was enclosed and distant and full of doors through which one went out and in until one found the door that led to this. It was so simple that she breathed in the simplicity, in the pain, as one breathes in the dawn — a Maytime dawn frosted with blossom.

Scatter the flowers. Scatter the flowers. There would be no flowers on his tomb. No rites. Only the priest behind the hangman.

She stood up and going to the wall opposite raised her hands high upon it. The warder turned and saw her and came towards her. She took down her hands and looked at him in such a way that the speech went mute on his lips.

She waited. She walked down the dim corridor and back again and down again and back. Redmond descended.

He took her hand. He held it so firmly that she had to submit.

'I must prepare you.' Valentine had asked him to say that. 'He is in another cell.'

'Thank you.' The change before death. Her father had been moved into the library. He had wanted his bed to be put there.

He let go her hand. 'There is another thing . . . .'

She waited. 'Yes.'

'You know that his brother, he has never believed that he did it? He still thinks that he is innocent. He is convinced that he is innocent.'

'I know that.' She knew quite well what he wanted. She said it for him. 'You want me to ask him?'

'If you could?'

'I will ask him.' She went up the stairs. He wished to come with her but she refused him. There would always be a warder to show her the way. He told her to walk down the corridor, past the cell in which Christy had been and that there would be somebody there to direct her. At the head of the stairs she looked down the long stone passage. She had not before realised its length because her eyes had never gone past Christy. It seemed to her as long as the whole building. Somebody suddenly turned on the electric light and as she walked she was aware of hidden peering eyes, of listening ears, of an underworld of awakened senses, and in front of her this lit stone way which shone like silver. A man came towards her. She did not look at him but through him. He meant nothing to her.

'Pardon me,' he was the governor, 'they told me you were here. If you will allow me I will show you where your son is.'

She thanked him. Bare thanks for the tone of his voice.

'I should like you to know how sorry I am. We have, you know, to obey instructions like everybody else.'

'Thank you.' He took her down more stone stairs and along another corridor that went back and back and shone like silver. Suddenly he put out his hand and said good-bye to her. He said 'you are there now' and told a warder to take her. For the brief part of a second she wondered where Valentine had got to. The warder went a pace or two, then bent down, barring her progress, and put a key into a lock. He stood upright again and she saw that she was to go in. The light emptied itself out of the corridor into her soul. Her soul was a flood of light, that made everything visible dark to her. She did not see Christy until she heard 'Mother,' and his arms went round her.

When she opened her eyes she saw that somebody had turned on a flashlight, two flashlights, and the first thing she saw in the cell was the open lavatory pan. She shut everything out again. 'Christy, my son, my son!' She opened her eyes again when his hands took her face and her gaze went direct into his, into the heavy load of sorrow in his eyes, into everlasting meaning.

Time and place were unsteadied in her. At last she said what she had meant to say, balancing the nearness of death: 'It might have been me, Christy, I might have been dying of some horrible disease. This good-bye would have to be said, this going out . . . they tell me that it will be over in a few seconds.'

'I am quite ready.'

Ah! he had found his right moment. 'And you are doing it for what you believe!' She remembered what Redmond had asked her. 'Did you do it, Christy?' She had to ask.

His arm went round her shoulders, gave her a special pressure. 'One of us did it. There were six of us. We were all guilty.'

She knew that he had not done it. He was one of the six.

He denied all action in her. 'They are not hanging me for murder, you know, but because I am a felon.'

His laughter was like a child's, triumphant, free. He was free. 'You are ready?' It was not a question but a belief in him.

'Quite. Only I'd rather have a rifle than a rope. Won't you sit down,' he indicated his bench, 'on my divan?'

Her smile lasted the fraction of a section and turned to tears on her, unshed tears. But she sat down. It was like sitting down at the Gates of Heaven.

'Valentine, did you know, Valentine of all people! He sent a telegram of abuse to the Home Secretary! They'll keep that out of the papers!'

She remembered the clerk slipping out of the office when she held the telegram in her hand that Redmond had given her.

Christy sat down close beside her, touching her. She felt the heat of his body. The heat of life. 'Do you know what

Cicely said to me . . . be good to her, Mother.'

'I will do everything that I can. I will take her with me, I shall go away, Christy . . . if she will come with me?'

'Where will you go to?'

'Out of the country, away . . . somewhere high and where I shall be a stranger. There is a place in Provence, desolate and high . . .' a perfect tomb of wars, wars of two thousand years ago. She would be a ghost there. A ghost of all the mothers whose sons had been taken. She belonged there. 'What did Cicely say?' They were like two people going away together remembering good-byes.

'She said that she would try to think of it . . . as a flock of birds, a flock of birds that would pass . . . and reach heaven. I did not know that you had told her that. It is a long time since I heard it . . . when I was a little child . . . .'

'When you were a little child.'

'Mother! It will only be a flock of birds . . . it will pass.'

'I know that it will pass.' Its meaning would never pass.

Whether somebody made a sign or not she never knew, but he stood up suddenly as though to attention. She stood up too and, for the last time, put her arms round him and her lips on his. 'Listen, Christy. I want you to take this in. All this night I shall keep vigil for you . . . on my knees.' She would shut herself into the hotel bedroom. 'I shall not stand up . . . until . . . until it is all over. I want you to dip into my soul, into my prayers and take courage from me. I will not fail you.'

'And I,' his voice was wrought for her and bound on her, 'I will not fail you. I will die like your son!'

Her pride was anguish. She did not know how she went out from him. A warder tried to take her arm in the silver brilliance of the corridor. 'Do you touch me!' she cried to him. He was a man in a dream to her, a spectre. She followed him in this dream into darkness, then through a door which opened on her into a deserted street. A street on which the night was falling. She walked on. She was alone in the twilit street, she and one man who was coming towards her. It was Valentine. 'Do you touch me!' she cried to him, and walked past him. He came up with her and took her arm, and walked with her. She could not prevent him.

'The car is here, Mother, at the corner. There is such a crowd . . . .' He waved an arm round the prison.

'Cicely!' she asked, 'where is Cicely?'

'She is there with the crowd, leading them . . . they are down on their knees, praying . . . .'

'Oh!' She was caught at last. She stopped. 'Take me . . . away!'

'Where shall I take you!'

Beyond the banners. Beyond the crowd on its knees. 'Take me,' she said steadily, 'to the little bedroom in the hotel.' She raised her face to the prison and from the prison to the sky above, the dark clouded chimera of the sky, the flying clouds of the night that had yet to come. 'What is that dark cloud in the sky?'

He offered comfort to her comfortless soul: 'It is going to rain.'

A smile widened her mouth: and she gave him back madness: 'It is only a flock of birds.'

The End

The Cards of the Gambler

Benedict Kiely

'An astonishing book.'
Thomas Flanagan, author of *The Year of the French*

to gamble — '*this is the desire that halts the heart, that sets the
soul swinging between fear of loss and hope of gain . . . .*'

Imaginative, mythical, fantastic, yet real — with *The
Cards of the Gambler* Benedict Kiely holds the reader as only
a great stroyteller can, weaving the ordinary and everyday
with gleaming threads of Irish folklore into the deep pattern
of a modern Faust.

It is the story of a Doctor who loses everything gambling
and thinks he is damned; who meets God in one pub and
Death in another, where a pact is made . . . .

Introduced by Thomas Flanagan, author of *The Year of the
French*, *The Tenants of Time* and *The End of the Hunt*.

ISBN 0 86327 477 3